BELONGING

Clairr O'Connor

Attic Press
Dublin

© Clairr O'Connor 1991

All rights reserved. Except for brief passages quoted in newspaper, magazine, radio or television reviews, no part of this book may be reproduced in any form or by any means, electronic or mechanical, including photocopying or recording, or by any information storage and retrieval systems without prior permission from the Publishers.

First published in Ireland in 1991 by
Attic Press
44 East Essex Street
Dublin 2

British Library Cataloguing in Publication Data
O'Connor, Clairr
    Belonging.
    I.   Title
    823.914 [F]
    ISBN 1-85594-014-0

Cover Design: Luly Mason
Origination: Attic Press
Printing: Billings & Sons Limited

The publishers acknowledge the assistance of The Arts Council/An Chomhairle Ealaíon who grant aided this book. The author was assisted by the Author's Royalty Scheme Loan of The Arts Council/An Chomhairle Ealaíon.

*For my sister, Ita,
and my cousins, Mary B and Eileen*

Thanks to the Tyrone Guthrie Centre, Annaghmakerrig, for residencies which supported this work.

CLAIRR O'CONNOR was born in Limerick and now lives in County Kildare with her family. Clairr O'Connor's plays have been produced on stage and radio in Ireland and the UK. Her short stories and poetry have appeared in numerous anthologies and journals. *When You Need Them*, her first collection of poetry, was published in 1989 by Salmon Press.

Contents

1 At Home *9*

2 Lies, Limerick and Hungary *69*

3 The Truth, such as it is *103*

4 A New Apartment *201*

1
AT HOME

'WRITE EVERYTHING DOWN,' Mark said. And I did. And I do. Sitting at Dad's old desk, obedient as a schoolgirl, my hands scrawl and race to tell all. Whatever that might be. I certainly don't know yet. His pipes, inkwell, fountain pen, letter-opener take my attention from time to time, but that's part of being back too. I look at them, touch them. I want them to be significant. In what way I'm not quite sure. They stand to attention like Stonehenge, relics of his past, while my cheap biro moves over the paper. I'm wearing one of Mam's black silk dresses, relieved, as she herself used to say, from the funereal look by the white lace collar.

The shutters are open and May lilac taps the window as I write. Cherry blossoms scatter the lawn, the wind lifting them. I move to and from the window-seat at intervals but I always take the brown leather journal with me. Or I slouch in the winged armchair, resting my head on the faded peacocks of the fabric. I have a flask and pour myself milky coffee. This does not keep Mrs Harty out but I can point to it when she intrudes. It shortens the time I have to talk to her.

Lists. I write them for comfort. Any list can look important. Number the list and you're on to a winner, at least for a little while. As a child, I admired Sam and

Marge's lists. They made one every day. Marge says they did it to please their mother, Aunt Anne, who was out at work all day and liked them to be busy. Later it became a habit.

I do not answer the doorbell after Mrs Harty goes home. I know these people mean well. At one point, in childhood, they were the pulse of my life, the boundaries of my existence. Relations, neighbours, my parents' friends. Who can believe in them now?

The funeral was a great success. Standing room only in the church. A mountain of wreaths, their sick sweetness, a jolly rouge, the last camouflage before the rot starts in earnest.

The pair of coffins, companionably side by side. Father Tom, stomach out and head thrown back, gave the final farewell, milking the pauses for dramatic effect. The congregation appreciated the performance. I was just as touched as everyone else. Mam and Dad taking the final bow together. Except they're not. Not my Mam and Dad, I mean.

Mark lives his life by the inane principle of maximising the positive and minimising the negative. He actually said to me on the phone, before I left New York, that my parents' death was a golden opportunity. Heaven sent! I could unload all that stuff that has been crowding out my head for years. Send it to lost luggage and move on. His last book was called *The Halo Effect of the Cliché*. You can see why.

I have been sleeping with this man, my therapist, for ten years. 'He should be struck off,' I hear you cry and you're right. In a crisis you hope for something more than a quotation.

I'm supposed to fly back to New York next Tuesday.

Back to Barry. Back to my students and dynamic summer courses. Back to Mark. But somehow I've lost the run of myself. Misplaced the bio or wandered into someone else's. Unable to place my head anywhere except here.

Here. Home. West Cork in May. The warmest May in Ireland that I can remember. My parents were not my parents so how can I be the person I thought I was? Barry was outraged when I rang him with the news. Our entire relationship is based on my ethnic authenticity. He fell in love with my Irish photograph albums. Me at five, in dancing costume of embroidered Celtic emblems, face widened by fat forced ringlets, legs made fragile by heavy patent dancing shoes. At seven, first communion veil adding six inches to my height, dress ballooned by stiff slips, one tooth missing, the upper lip attempting to hide the gap, succeeding only in a Bell's palsy grimace, all expression lost.

'You mean you're not Irish?'

'Looks that way.'

'Maybe the old man was loopy in the end. Just wrote this fantastic diary as a pastime.'

'He left it with the solicitor.'

There was a crashing silence after that. I don't know about you but I've never been able to allow for pauses on transatlantic calls. Usually, I'm in such thrifty excitement that I talk too fast and end up having to repeat everything.

I know he's upset. I can tell by his breathy confusion but I know he won't admit it. Barry's like that. He holds things in tightly, except in bed — but that's a different story.

'Dee, it will be alright.' His voice is low and

controlled. I feel my guts twist and there's a damp patch between my legs. He was here on holidays with me last year. We made the yellow room our own after Mam and Dad had settled down to sleep for the night. Sneaking our way to intimacy excited me just as much as the act itself. Wanting this man has been both the centre and also the main confusion in my life.

'How can it be alright?' I scream. 'I don't even know who I am. How can it be alright?'

He's patient. 'I'll write. You're in shock. We'll work it through.'

'Will you shut up?'

'Okay, maybe I shouldn't have said that. Just don't write one of your crazy letters.'

I'm so angry by now, I'm volcanic.

'Crazy letters! What's that supposed to mean?'

'Honey, I didn't mean anything. You'll be home next week. We can talk then.'

'You should be here! I'll write as many goddamn letters as I please.'

'You said you wanted to go back on your own. Remember. Less to worry about that way, you said.'

'That was then. This is now. Everything's changed. I'm Hungarian, for Christ's sake.'

'Hysteria isn't going to change anything,' he reasons. 'Culturally and by rearing, you're Irish.'

'I'm a fraud, an impostor.'

I slam down the phone. Right now I hate Barry even though I know I love him. On reflection, I realise 'fraud' and 'impostor' are words that I should never say to Barry. Even about myself. He believes totally in the biography he has fabricated for himself, a life he has forged against all the odds. Doubt has become foreign to him. Mark says I validate my life through conflict and contradiction. At an earlier stage in our relationship when I actually used to listen to him properly, he persuaded me that anger was my spur, indignation my fuel.

Mrs Harty comes in every day as if Mam and Dad are still here. But what do I call them now? She clumps about the house, as always, imposing order. The house, genuine Georgian, if somewhat shabby, is shelved. Generally speaking, I've noticed that some houses tend to shelving and clutter and others to smooth surfaces and blank walls. The shelves groan here under books, ornaments, plants, old newspapers, endless back issues of magazines, cameras put down for a moment that can never be picked up again, at least not by them.

Yesterday I screamed but the hoover was in full throttle and Mrs Harty didn't hear. Truth is, I don't know what to do with my new found knowledge and the nervous energy it has generated is frightening. Seems like I've been pacing since I came. From room to room, touching furniture and objects. The feel of a book spine, the curl of velvet cushions. Maybe if I could cry? But I'm too angry for that yet. Yesterday, I smashed the gaudy Madonna, the souvenir I lugged all the way on the bus from Knock at the tender age of ten. In this house of Madonnas, who'd miss it? Dad put it right next to his collection of silver snuff boxes on the tallboy and praised it extravagantly. I didn't know then that ugly things depressed him and religious objects of devotion made him uneasy. He must have loved me to place it where he did. I tell myself I must finish reading the journal. But how can I? Only a small part of it is in English. It is in four parts, or, at least in four shabby copybooks. One has newspaper cuttings from the 1950s, another has a small group of photographs from Hungary. The third one is written in a foreign language, presumably Hungarian, and the fourth one is in English, thoughts and observations Dad jotted down. The gist of this mishmash, at least from what I can make out, is that my 'real mother' was Hungarian. Some of the jottings read:

A Hungarian mother
Leave well enough alone

The questions torment me. Why was she Hungarian? Where is she now? Why did she abandon me? Why did nobody ever tell me? Not even a hint. I keep the journal by me. A clumsy thing. Large and rectangular, four copybooks encased in an old-fashioned brown leather binding. Did Dad keep it in his desk in the study? That's where he did his writing. Aunt Em used to tease him about his great unfinished novel. That seems centuries ago now. I thought it was a joke. I sent them all away after the wake. They said they understood but I could see that they didn't. Marge keeps ringing, making solicitous inquiries. I want to know all the answers but something holds me back from finishing the journal, though I know I'll have to in the end. My appetite's disappeared. Gone underground. At least by day. Everything tastes chalky. I pretend to eat to please Mrs Harty. Always too thin for her liking, she worries about me losing weight. Yesterday, I rolled two lamb chops in my napkin and dumped them when she had gone.

I can't go out. Not to the village anyway. Too many faces to talk to. I keep thinking — how many of them know? Does Mrs Harty? How about the Brady sisters in the post office? And what about cousins and relatives? Strictly speaking, we're not connected and never were. And what about Sam?

It turns out we could have done what we nearly did that summer in the cave after all. Cousinhood and lack of expertise inhibited us. I still dream about it: the darkness of the cave, our wet t-shirts, the moist abyss of mouths.

And the will. Mr Fogarty, white hair overshooting his bi-focals, elocuting each syllable in deep baritone, 'To our darling and only daughter, Deirdre' . . . and after all the legalities he hands me the brown paper package with the journal.

'Your dad said you were to have this too.' Did he know what was in it? Was he only pretending he didn't? They hand you grenades and they smile. These days anything is possible. Everything tidy and in order in the will. Then the package. An innocuous brown package tied with twine. Like the packages I brought home from the butcher's as a child, liver or chops inside. This time though the guts, the entrails of my origins. Maybe Barry is right and it's a mad, final derangement. A fantasy that Dad nourished in a journal, then put in a brown package and gave to Fogarty. But he was never unkind. Courteous and entertaining when pushed into contact with people but with a preference for his own company even within the family.

When I summon him, I see him in the greenhouse admiring his tomatoes or smiling at the dinner table having forced down one of Mam's concoctions on Mrs Harty's day off. Always smiling. And if he spoke at all, it was to give compliments whether they had been earned or not.

He was gentle. Mam was quiet. There was little conversation in our house. We met at mealtimes and spent evenings together in the sitting room but we followed our own interests. We didn't take pleasure in talk for talk's sake. We hoarded words carefully, taking them out and dusting them down on appropriate occasions when politeness demanded. I became a talker, later, in adulthood.

Now I am positively spendthrift, throwing words to the wind, appropriately or not. Mark says I pepper my conversation with small blasphemies to show that I have freed my tongue from constricted beginnings. When I think of childhood, I think of silence. That time returns like a soundless movie. At least that was the sepia memory until the explosive brown package arrived. Now everyday life is a grenade not yet thrown.

The house is quiet except for Mrs Harty's daily ministrations. Greta says:

'Forget the hieroglyphics, kid. Life is too short. Sometimes you get lost only because you follow the road signs.'

But Greta isn't here and besides she has been known to run to and from disasters at an alarming pace, even by her own standards. Her hectic vitality saves her from the cave of depression. She will not admit defeat, at least not by another human being. She faces disasters squarely and accepts all blame. She says it's easier that way. When her second husband, Ben, ran off with an opera singer, she reasoned she had brought it on herself by dragging him to the opera when he didn't want to go. Mussorgsky's 'Khovanschina' signalled the end of Greta's second marriage.

How can I put the place up for sale and wing my way back to New York? Greta says it's easy. You hand the property over to an estate agent and then you book a ticket on a plane. Just like I did when I was twenty-one. Those first few weeks in New York, Greta and I had such fun. We stayed in the Algonquin for a week. Toasted each other at the blue bar, lost the coded card that was the room key and read Dorothy Parker poems aloud at night. We queued for cheap theatre tickets at Times Square at three o'clock in the afternoon, having spent the morning before in a queue at the Lincoln Centre for opera tickets. Our energy and enthusiasm for culture was boundless. How long ago that seems now!

Greta really lost her patience with me when I telephoned her yesterday.

'What the hell are you paying Mark for? He's been dissecting your little life for ten years. He diagnosed boredom and an exaggerated fear of loud sounds and sex. And now when something really exciting has happened you want to go to pieces. I wish someone would give me a clean slate to start over.'

Like all children, I had nurtured the fantasy that really I was adopted and that some day more dynamic, exciting parents would turn up to claim me. So much for wishes.

We punish ourselves for what we are and for what we aren't. All the Irish national neuroses I claimed naturally, have they to be abandoned now? A Hungarian mother? I barely know where the country is. When I was at school we had Cold War nuns. We were familiar with the Iron Curtain, having no idea what it was but knowing for certain it was appalling, sinful, mentioned in prayers for the sad Christians imprisoned behind it.

Dad 'turned' to marry Mam. A reticent man by nature, he was doubly cautious in the presence of Catholic clergy. They hadn't exactly welcomed the new convert with open arms. He was most himself in the presence of his few elderly Protestant cousins and his sisters, Em and Alice, who lived with us. Somehow, their laughter and silences coincided.

Dad was fifty when I was born and Mam forty-five. Apart from the Harty children and Marge and Sam I was surrounded by adults two generations ahead of me. Embroidery and lace weighed down my childhood. I was never scolded if I muddied my dresses but I seldom did. I seemed to have been born careful, always on the look-out to keep unpleasantness at bay. My photo albums show me at the piano at six: smile, ringlets, and hands arranged to perfection. I was a dull musician, unrelentingly adequate, yet I was invited to play every Sunday evening for my parents and my two aunts. They clapped enthusiastically at the end.

I touched the piano yesterday but could not map out the careful tunes preserved in the fingertips. I know those tunes still. I've played them all through my adult life on strange pianos when forced to do a turn at parties but somehow on this piano, so upright and heavy, with its nicotined keys, I couldn't play. Even childhood tunes seem an impersonation.

I keep remembering precise things and racing about the house to verify them. Yesterday I recalled in perfect detail the cloth on my dressing table when I was ten, white linen, starched stiffly, with white racing rabbits embroidered along the edges. By the time Mrs Harty arrived the entire contents of the linen cupboard were on the floor and I hadn't succeeded in finding it.

'Chest of drawers in your room, third one from the end, like always,' she said, stepping over the debris. 'Death takes people funny. Some like to gather everything up and others like to clear everything out.'

And it was there too. The bunnies still chasing each other, the edges a little frayed. I lay down on the bed and put it over my eyes and I must have slept because the next thing I knew, Mrs Harty was standing over me with a lunch tray.

'Marge rang, said she wanted to come out for lunch but I told her you were sleeping.'

'Thanks, Mrs Harty. You're an angel.'

'No, I'm not and you're not going to keep to yourself for too much longer. She's thinking of ringing Dr Greene to have a look at you.'

'Why?'

'I suggested it when she said she was worried.'

'Thanks a bundle.'

'It wouldn't do any harm to get yourself looked at.'

'I'm not an exhibition piece.'

'You're a bundle of nerves. A good tonic and a few pills to make you sleep off the shock, that's what you need.'

'I just want to be on my own.'

'So did Larry Power and he wasn't happy until he was dangling from an apple tree, abandoning poor Maisie like that. We don't want any of that class of behaviour here and this place full of trees.'

'I'm not the hanging type, Mrs Harty.'

But now that she's mentioned the possibility of destruction, I'm beginning to entertain ideas on the subject. Maybe I should see Dr Greene and start hoarding tranquillizers, just to reassure myself of the possibility.

I was six when it happened. I missed Larry, missed him in his horse and trap, cap askew, churns clanking, waving a shy hello on his way to the creamery. I knew the apple trees were to blame, that's all. It put me off apples for a while until my childish greed overcame my fear.

'Where's Maisie now?' I ask Mrs Harty.

'Same place she's been for years, inside that clatter of a house talking to herself, her wild cats tearing the last bit of stuffing from the furniture. Your Mam and Dad always said you were highly strung. Maybe you should see Dr Greene as Marge says. My conscience couldn't bear unnatural acts.'

'I'm perfectly fine, Mrs Harty. The shock of a double death, jet lag, that's all.'

'The best parents a child could wish for. That's what they were. You wanted for nothing and neither did I. Good employers. If it wasn't for them I don't know how I'd have managed with Harty and his back and a houseful of children to feed. Decent people. Such a delicate woman, Mrs Pender. It was a wonder she lasted as long as she did. All those miscarriages early on and then her condition as well.'

'What condition?' I force calm on the question even though panic pulses my head.

'It's not right to be talking about the dead,' she sniffs. 'Things weren't much talked about then. Backs are a different matter.'

I grew up with Harty's back. Her husband of decades, the father of her ten children, she has never called him anything but Harty.

They met while she toiled in the Major's kitchen and Harty worked on the Major's land. One day Harty toppled from the Major's tractor. Unfit for work, he was dismissed. Those were the brute days before liability or compensation.

She left the Major's kitchen after Harty proposed. Dad gave them the cottage to live in and in return she came to do for us. Harty did the odd job about the place when his back allowed and she's never scolded or criticised him in my memory, tending his back during her many pregnancies, dismissing her own pains as 'natural'.

Maybe Greta gets her stoicism from her mother. Never mind the obvious differences — Harty has been Mrs Harty's only man, her devotion as enduring as the bog. She wields her protective armour around him and shouts down his critics with a cry that's blood curdling. A warrior queen. Greta, her patience and strengths tried by another culture, has to all intents and purposes become an American, taken on the camouflage, the guerrilla uniform and slapstick of the urban survivor, yet she remains her mother's daughter in the face of adversity, cocking a snook at her own Majors, refusing to let anyone colonise her pain.

'She couldn't help her fits, no more than Harty could help his back.'

We're back on course again but it's an alarming one. 'Fits! I don't remember any fits.'

'You weren't allowed to see them. They hadn't the

pills for it back then, you see. I'd stick a spoon in her mouth so she wouldn't swallow her tongue and Mr Pender would talk to her real gentle. Though I don't think she could hear what he said. He talked so quietly. Her eyes would be rolling everywhere. Sure, isn't it a blessing it's all behind her now.'

'Epilepsy?'

'That's right. But it wouldn't matter what it was called. Something fierce it was and her living in permanent dread of it. It wasn't so bad later on when there were pills for it. The suffering that woman went through no one will know.'

'Amazing what you can hide from a child!'

'They didn't want you frightened or upset.'

'Or enlightened?' I say before I can stop myself.

'I'll have none of that smart talk. They wouldn't like it. You're as bad as my Greta with your tongue when you put your mind to it. Gentle decent souls. They always acted for the best.' She picks up the lunch tray and is on her way out with it.

'Marge will be here for tea.' She throws the words over her shoulder before I can object.

Marge will be here for tea. Down through the years the knowledge that Marge would be here for tea was wonderful news. Now all I feel is annoyance.

Marge and Sam. Brother and sister. Marge and Sam and Deirdre. Cousins. My only cousins. Special people, special times. Tea on our own. Just Mrs Harty smiling over the scones, cakes, jampots. Greta bursting in to join us if her indignation allowed.

'You don't want the likes of me about with those precious cousins here talking la-di-da.'

'Of course I do,' I'd protest, afraid she'd come and

afraid she wouldn't.

'It's alright for you to issue invitations but it's my Ma has to do the skivvying.'

'Yes, I know,' I'd blush my confusion and embarrassment, 'but Marge and Sam's father is dead. We're luckier than them.'

Having pointed out our superiority on the father front she'd relent graciously.

'Okay, I'll come then but no fancy talk from you, I'm warning you.'

Fancy talk from me could be as little as saying 'thank you,' when Marge and Sam passed a plate my way. If Greta was in generous mood, her impatience wouldn't burst forth until she'd filled her face with goodies. Then, her energies stoked, she'd play too boisterously in the yard or the orchard, deliberately tripping Marge or Sam, preferably both.

Her bad behaviour at the table had to be covert because her mother was tending us. But this didn't deter her. I was kicked or pinched as often as circumstance would allow. The odd squeak emerged from me at times but these I suppressed. I knew what was good for me. To be fair, Greta behaved like this only when there were other people with us. On our own, she was an entertaining companion, full of ideas for games and stories.

'You know Mrs Mannion, her with the snotty-nosed brats near the railway. Well, the auntie in England sent them two gorgeous pink nylon dresses with stiff slips and what do you think the hard hearted bitch did?'

She'd pause for dramatic effect and I'd shake my head and say I couldn't guess.

'Cut them up for dusters and her with a filthy house

that's never been dusted before. Sheer badness, that's what I call it.'

I'd nod solemnly, her adult-sounding tongue stunning me with its vigour.

'And do you know her brother? The one who works in the pottery, with the limp. He's going to have to marry that ugly Costello one, the fat one with glasses.'

'Why?'

'Why what?'

'Why has he to marry her?'

'Because she didn't get that fat on her own.' She'd laugh and run off.

Life and the facts about it came naturally to Greta. She passed on the titbits to me and I worried out their meaning long after she'd danced her way across the fields to home.

Marge and Sam. Twins. Identical blonde heads leaning together over a jigsaw. They rarely fought, a fact Greta found sinister and weird.

'It would be natural to belt each other from time to time. Smarmy brats!'

My only cousins. Cousins no more. Summer holidays when they came to stay. Sharing a room with Marge. Sam in the attic. Homemade lemonade. Sandals and summer bonnets that Marge and I pushed aside when Mam wasn't looking. Lazy or bad-tempered bouts of tennis with Greta. Dad reading *Alice in Wonderland* aloud. Mam and Aunt Anne sewing together, the tut-tut of the black and gold Singer sewing machines ticking away their hours.

Marge and Sam. Same generous mouth and oriental eyes. Skin that burned pink, never brown like mine. The two of them streaked with Calamine lotion on a picnic rug on the beach. Happy days. What am I supposed to do with those images now?

I adored Marge but I burned with love for Sam. The toss of his head and the way he held a tennis racquet. His lazy laugh, creamy teeth. Tongue, a blatant red, a host, inviting. We kissed once only, that time in the cave, caught in a summer storm. Wet through and suddenly cold, we clung together for warmth. I kissed him. I'd been imagining it for too long not to do it. Then we were both inexpertly pushing lips and discovering tongues. A clap of thunder cymballed our triumph. He pushed me away gently and said, 'We're cousins.'

And so we were, for years. Not now. Other people have cousins to spare but there's never been anyone but Sam and Marge for me. First cousins. Dad's two sisters, Aunt Alice and Aunt Em, had never married and all his Protestant relatives were in retirement by my teen years, their children on the first rung of middle age. Sam, Aunt Anne's pride and joy. An accountant in South Africa. Mam shared her delight. I shared my disappointment and frustration with no one, not even Marge. Certainly not Greta. My torture would have been guaranteed. No, I cried into years of pillows and persuaded myself by my twenties that it had been the usual teenage crush.

I cry to myself now in an excess of pity in my childhood bed, Mrs Harty noising the kitchen into order below me. Familiar sounds. I might never have left. I concentrate on the faded balloons of wallpaper. Smile at the teddies, the chipped china doll sets, the photographs of my Leaving Cert class, Mam and Dad holding me stiffly on my first birthday, Marge and me sharing the swing in the back garden, Dad with his prize tomatoes in the greenhouse. Deirdre, Dee, that's me, Dad's little girl, Barry's little colleen, a total fraud.

What's the national costume of Hungary?

* * *

The weight of the blankets wakes me. Mam had never warmed to duvets. Woollen blankets, crisp white linen, those were proper bedclothes and that was the beginning and end of it. Polyester patterns never made an entrance here. Electric blankets were allowed but hot water bottles were preferred. She mended the sheets herself, deftly patching wear and tear, white mountains of linen, chattering through the sewing machine. And it was invisible to the eye. Only a toe deliberately seeking a patch when sleep did not come, discerned a slight variation in texture.

I'm sweating, the sheets in fretful mounds about me. The shutters lock out light, only thin lines of it gaining entrance. I'm lying on a bump, something that isn't a tangle of blankets. I feel about and retrieve the half-eaten apple I munched last night. Night hungers. There is something about this house that brings them on. I can't eat by day and spend much of the time hiding the food Mrs Harty prepares for me. But in the small hours I'll eat any junk: chocolate, cake, biscuits, cheese. Probably feeding my own night horrors. I eat fast and with a compulsion that's unstoppable. I've always been thin. 'Skinny,' Mrs Harty says. Never moved above seven and a half stone no matter what I ate.

Mark says, how, when and what you eat, are good indicators of your self esteem. Well, take a good look now, buddy! I'm in my childhood bedroom, lying on half-eaten apples, a tray on the floor holds the detritus of two mugs of hot chocolate. Wafers float in the remains of a winged banana split. Three empty papers of Mars bars complete the scene. Marge and I had a midnight feast. I ate most of it. She's sleeping almost soundlessly in the other bed by the window, having been afraid to leave me alone last night after my outburst. She would have preferred to have gone home to Tom and the twins. I listened in on the extension.

'She's been reading some of Uncle's writing and she's convinced it's . . . that it's some sort of horrible diary.'

'What! Isn't a man entitled to some privacy?'

'He gave it to Fogarty for her.'

'Oh! But is it necessary to stay overnight?' He's peeved.

'She's been on her own too much. It will give us a chance to talk.'

'Talk? About what?'

'I don't know. We'll see. Some of it is in a foreign language.'

'What?'

'The diary . . . the journal, but it's disturbed her.'

'Death disturbs everyone but you'd think Deirdre would be pleased that they both went within a day of each other. I'd like to go like that.'

'I'll have to go, Tom. Kiss Rachel and Simon for me.' Tom and Marge, Rachel and Simon. Lucky people. Happy family. They know who they are and love each other.

I pay Mark to tell me who I am but I don't believe him. I mostly lie when I'm on his couch. It's all a nonsense. I understand that when Mark says even noncommunication communicates something. Funny, he assumes my silences are benign, a communion of breaths, so to speak. When I get right down to it, I know that I should stop the sessions. But I don't. I look forward to the ritual of pretend passion. I draw on the details for comfort. I am in Mark's office. The session is over. I may have talked or not according to inclination. If I have talked it's invention. Little titbits that I know will please him and cost me nothing because I know them to be false.

Lying on the wide black couch, its leather warming to my touch, I talk at the white walls, never connecting with Mark's eyes. I look at the walls. I pick over the large abstract painting that hangs on the opposite wall. It's splashed with virulent yellow, nuclear red and the blackness of night. Sometimes I fancy I'm really talking to the men and women I see whirling in abstraction on the canvas. Other times I concentrate on the burning flames licking the night sky to the right.

When I finish talking, I close my eyes for a moment. Then I stand up and pull my skirt off roughly. Only then do I kick off my shoes and pull down my tights. Just as I'm about to step out of them, Mark will grab me from behind, preventing me. We bend down together, gently pull the tights to their full length.

I turn towards him. We're holding the tights like a skipping rope. We pull towards each other carefully as if measuring the distance between us. Torso to torso, we drop the tights and I unstrip him carefully, starting with his jacket, right down to his socks until he's naked, ready.

I untie my top briskly. I don't wear a bra. Mark lies on the octagonal rug, blue-greens. I straddle him. He enters me. As I ride I call out to the men and women trapped in the painting.

I slept with Big Ted and White Rabbit last night, making my final selection at the very last minute not to hurt the feelings of the rest when I gently, as if by accident, slid them to the floor. The brown journal is under the pillow.

'Morning, Marge,' I say softly, not really expecting an answer. Marge has always been a deep sleeper.

No answer. I'm relieved. I shouldn't have made a scene last night. That was the first time this house ever heard a raised voice. Marge grew up in a muted household too and she hasn't had ten years of Mark's attentions urging her to express herself. 'Getting in touch with the real you,' as he says. Marge was stunned last night...

We sit either side of the fireplace in the living room, the sherry bottle at half level, Chopin's ballads clichéing our peace. I don't talk much at first, just empty my glass steadily. Marge talks. This and that, neutral talk. As I listen, anger quickens. Shared memories. She's shaking them like a child's rattle to comfort and amuse. Then she moves on to Rachel's music, Simon's biology experiments, Tom's new line in vases for export. Aunt Em and Aunt Alice, their tea parties for distressed Protestant gentlewomen. When we were girls, Marge and I handed around the sandwiches. Thin sandwiches on thin china. A lifetime of good deeds and good humour behind them, restrained elegance their calling card.

'Dad and Mam weren't my parents at all. Can you credit that?' I slur the question, rudely interrupting a tale of Rachel's amazing rendition of some piece or other. I haven't been listening. Marge has been driving on steadily bumper to bumper, while I've let familiarity flow over me as comforting and deadening as a list of directions. Impatient for a break in the traffic, I dive in, a hardy pedestrian, thumbs up at the 'Don't walk' sign, cars screeching to a halt.

'You're upset. Easy to make mistakes when we're in shock. Uncle wrote for recreation. That's all there is to it.' Marge and Sam always called him Uncle. Never Uncle John. This formality enlivens my rage. 'For Christ's sake, he had a name even if he wasn't my Dad.'

A red blotch of embarrassment colours her neck but curiously does not climb her face.

'Please, you mustn't.'

'Mustn't what?'

She drops her voice, as if to step back from even this mild protest.

'Bad language, anger, it will do no good.'

I do not take kindly to convenient dumbness, however eloquent. I have paid heavily on the other side of the Atlantic to have my tongue loosened.

'I will speak.' Anger makes me hoarse. 'If you don't want to hear then go home to Tom and the children.'

I walk out the open French windows and look in at Marge from the terrace. I have become something I never was, a petulant teenager, waving the red rag at a parent. Highly inappropriate and decades too late but I cannot stop myself. The first slab of crazy paving laid, I rush skittishly on, anxious to complete my handiwork, to remake the summer terrace of childhood.

'How can any of you be the same to me now? Nothing has changed for you yet everything has changed for me. Can't you see that? You are not my cousin. How do you feel about that? Do you feel anything at all?'

I have planted manic gnomes on the terrace. They run amok, grimacing, showing bums and thumbing thumbs. One of them pees loudly, a giant penis hosing Marge while he tips a toothless grin at me.

I realise that I am standing over Marge, the delicate sherry glass draining its contents on her white dress. She does not move or speak. I put the glass on one of the oak tables that scatter the room. I daub her dress with an ineffectual tissue, wiping in the stickiness. Still she does not speak. Tears almost fall from her green almond eyes but she does not touch her face or turn it from me.

The cries torn from my throat fill the room. Marge stands to startled attention as if she can't quite figure the source of the noise. Then a memory takes hold. She does not move closer but sings softly,

'Daydums, Deedums, Deirdre, Dee. She's where the sun begins for me. Daydums, Deedums, Deirdre, Dee.'

One of Dad's favourite nonsense songs for me. I sit back in my chair again. Marge sits down too. She refills our glasses. I toss it back. Nausea twists my gut. I have spoken loudly and out of turn. The words cannot be taken back. Yet I feel that this is just the beginning, the first forced entry to this deaf house. I touch a loose tile. Cardinal red. Octagonal. Looking down I realise I have no shoes on.

I cannot remember taking them off. Did I put them on at all? So many summers spent barefoot on this terrace, or in Bluebell field, Horse field, the orchard or the summer house. Greta and me, our legs nut-brown, our dresses pulled into the elastic of our knickers playing 'Boating, boating up the canal'. Marge and Sam, hair almost white from the sun, shoes, socks and hats on to shield their fairness, reading or smiling that smile, indulgent, even then, in charge, like adults.

I move indoors to the gilt mirror above the mantleshelf, anxious to see myself. Marge is still singing very softly, the tune muted to the serenity of a lullaby. I do not recognise myself. The mirror is stained. Patterns I know well. But there is something missing. My hair. Long, black, swishing my waist. It's gone. My hair stands, a spiky halo, crudely cut, its jagged edges reaching upwards in a cartoon terror.

'My hair!' I am pulling at it now, as if by magic it will elasticate to its usual length.

'You cut it,' she says quietly, holding my gaze as she talks.

And so I had. In an excess of temper, I had taken the kitchen scissors to my black hair and cut savagely without benefit of mirror or hairdresser. My vanity of vanities, gone. Savaged by my own hand after I listened to Marge and Tom on the extension. The inevitability of their happiness pierced me to the quick. While I was perched on the cliff edge of loss and dementia, they were exchanging news of me like so much small change. I'd show them. And I did. Chopped and hacked until the dining room floor shone with the dead ravens of my locks. How could I have forgotten that so easily? Marge's shock when she came through the door, her cheeks blanching and her sudden collapse. She reached towards the table and plucked the damask cloth in her fist, taking with her Mrs Harty's tea.

I leave her casually lying in the debris of tea things

and view her from above. Let her come round in her own time, I think. But I know that this is only a sop to my cruel streak. She is soon struggling to her feet again. I get the sherry bottle and decide to skip tea and so we sit side by side, beginning to talk. Family matters, safe territory. Later, upstairs, we pretend jollity, the salve of girlhood jokes rediscovered, to heal the evening burns. Chocolate mugs in hand, we reclaim that territory. Teddies on either side, we sprawl and trawl the safe waters of our long ago. My stutter, her sunburns. Safely sealed by time, we can laugh at them now, their remote tortures flying from us. Sam is here in his long short pants, busily bending Meccano to his will. Greta shakes her curls and fists in fury as she prances out of the summerhouse. I talk, the babble of childhood crowding the room, the mind blanketed with fatigue. I do not remember falling asleep.

Marge must have closed the shutters. I follow their thin lines, the light sneaking through. I listen to her breathing, willing her to wake. But she doesn't and I cannot stay still. Energised anew by desolation, I scrabble with the bedclothes and tiptoe from the room.

* * *

'Two grown women and the place left like a pigsty.'
'Morning, Mrs Harty.'
'There's some queer fashions around these days. All I can say is, thank God the funeral is over, not to be parading yourself in public like a poorly feathered bird. Who scalped you?'
'I cut it myself. Marge is still asleep.'

'I only hope that she sorted out all the peculiarities.' She dusts the sideboard exaggeratedly as she speaks.

'Peculiarities?'

'Don't box clever with me. You know exactly what I mean . . . moping indoors and carrying that book around with you all the time.'

'Mrs Harty, I'm sorry about the mess in the dining room but Marge fainted and . . .'

'Fainted! Have you been tormenting that poor girl?'

'She's sleeping,' I say again, in an attempt to ward off ferocity.

'Must be the shock.'

'Shock?'

'She's .always been sensitive. The funeral and the way you're carrying on. No wonder she's worn out.'

'Marge has always been a deep sleeper, just like Greta.'

'Greta may sleep long and deep alright but never with the same partner for too long. Of course Harty doesn't know the half of it. He's too sensitive for complications.'

We both gaze reflectively out the kitchen window in the direction of their cottage, though it's two fields away, as if we're checking Harty's sensitivity.

'You'll have to have a good breakfast then. Women eat too little these days. You're not on a diet, are you?' She stares me squarely in the face. 'Some people will resort to anything to hide the fact that they're not eating.'

'I don't have time for that kind of nonsense.' I wonder if somehow she's found the food I've hidden. 'My life's too busy for diets. We took a tray of goodies up with us last night.'

Pleased, she sets about breakfast and my stomach curdles at the thought. My only chance is waking Marge. Her appetite has always been enormous.

'I'll bang the bell when it's ready,' she says as I round the corner for the door.

The bell, a monstrous green-black, colours it has accreted with age, is an old bell from the pottery which, in grandfather Daniel's day, the manager used to ring every morning at eight o'clock to summon the workers. A simple ugly handbell, it's been on the kitchen window nearest to the pantry as long as I can remember. Mrs Harty will clang her revenge for last night's breakages.

I go back to Marge. She's still shuttered in dreams. I'm alarmed at the state of the room. Even in the half light, the disarray seems rampant. Photo albums lie scattered on my old school desk. Chronology has been disrupted. Grandad Daniel, a man dead before I had time to remember him, smiles severely side by side with Greta in a school production of 'Messiah,' Barry on a St Patrick's Day parade, Sam in his office in Africa.

Two bookcases lean to one side, the weight of their contents forcing them to waltz. The two wardrobes, doors winging space, have nothing hanging in them. Clothes of all sorts, jeans, T-shirts, suits, dresses are plaited in an intricate pile on the floor. I pull and tug, unearth a blouse and skirt. It's a wonder that Marge's fastidious nature allowed her to sleep in such bedlam last night. 'Marge,' I shake her gently. The eyes forced open are still fuzzy with sleep. It's clear that she does not know where she is.

'Tom?'

'No. You're at Uncle's.'

The bell clanging makes Marge jump.

'Good God! What's that?' Worry lines pave her forehead.

'Mrs Harty is extracting her pound of flesh for last night's carry-on. It's Grandfather's bell. We're being summoned to a full Irish breakfast, as they say.'

'I'm quite hungry,' she admits sheepishly.

'Good. You'll have to manage most of mine as well. I can only eat at night these days.'

'What if she stands over us like she used to?'

'Improvise. We'd better clean our plates. I'm sorry about last night.'

'What about Dr Greene?'

'I've no need of him.'

She doesn't believe me.

'I'm doing okay. I'm not fully myself, whatever that's supposed to be, but I'm in no danger.'

'But...'

'I have to work things out my own way, that's all. I'll need more time here but that's alright. I can get my classes covered. I'll ask if I need help. I promise.' My tone is brisk, businesslike, an attempt to distance myself from last night's madwoman with the scissors.

'We'd better eat,' I urge Marge.

'Before washing?' she says, alarmed.

'Face and hands will do. You can have a bath after. I can't face the groaning board alone.'

I open the shutters energetically as if this makes a proper start to the day. In the kitchen Mrs Harty is determined to play matron and headmistress. 'I'll start you off with creamed porridge and fruit,' she plods from Aga to table with steaming bowls, but her talk flows on.

Her eyes take in Marge's bowl the moment it empties and this propels her back towards the oven. I've been moving the blobs of porridge about, raising a spoon to my mouth any time she's looked my way. I seize my chance and spoon half of mine into Marge's bowl. Unperturbed, she starts eating again.

Back at table Mrs Harty sets down two plates of rashers, sausages, eggs, black and white pudding and tomatoes.

'A wonderful breakfast, Mrs Harty,' Marge compliments her.

'I forgot the hot scones and you'll have some toast.'

'I don't know how you do it, Mrs Harty. Your brown bread melts in the mouth. I make it exactly to your recipe and it never tastes the same. Rachel and Simon nag me about it all the time.'

'I'll give you a loaf to bring home to them.' She heads to the oven again. I offload rashers and sausages on Marge. A trail of squashed tomato marks my route.

'Harty and myself got a card from Sam last week. He's doing great work out there.'

Exploiting the black people of Africa, I think, but I don't say it aloud. She marshals toast on the toast rack. 'Must be a hardship for him though. That heat all the time and him with the same skin as yourself.' She clucks sympathetically at Marge, then looks at me closely and examines my plate.

'You're eating a bit better this morning. But not a pick of pudding has passed your lips, I see.'

'I've never liked black or white pudding but the rest was delicious.'

'I hope you've knocked some sense into her, Marge. She's been roaming the house disturbing things. If she told me what she's looking for, like that tablecloth the other day, I'm sure I'd know where to find it.'

Her voice is teetering on the edge of tears but to the best of my knowledge I've never seen Mrs Harty cry. I want to prevent that at all costs.

'You've helped a lot, Mrs Harty. More than can be expected in fact and I do appreciate it.'

Too late I realise they're the wrong words.

'Don't talk to me about appreciation.' She flops into a chair at the table.

I know then she's really upset because she has always refused to sit while we were eating.

'I know my place and I'd prefer to keep it, Mrs Pender,' she'd say with a whiff of disapproval at Mam. She used to pick up hints on what she called 'proper behaviour' from magazines. She had amassed recipes from the same source. These she cut out carefully and pasted into her cookery scrapbook.

'I've had the height of appreciation from your parents, Deirdre. No one could ask for better. All my girls done out in lace for the first communion. Not to talk about the wedding dresses and veils. And my own kitchen dresser filled with the best cups and plates from the pottery. And now to be left the cottage and acre!'

'Uncle told you all about that, Mrs Harty,' Marge intervenes. 'He wanted you to be secure. You've earned anything you got.'

'Of course you have,' I add, glad that Marge has taken charge.

'That's alright then. As long as I know, but the way you've been pulling things apart around here, I thought maybe that . . .'

'Been too much on her own lately, that's all, Mrs Harty. We're going for a nice brisk walk now and I'm going to insist she comes over for dinner tomorrow night. A bit of exercise does wonders.'

I'm grateful to Marge. The Head Girl never shows indecision even if she feels it. Mrs Harty is not going to cry now. The ferocity of her domestic intent breaks out again.

'I'll do out the pantry shelves today. They need a going over,' and she's on her feet.

* * *

In shorts and T-shirts we set out, Marge an Israeli freedom fighter in khaki, myself a clash of colour and patterns, swirls of reds, greens and yellows. I can't ever remember early May as warm or sunny as this. There's a black and white photograph in an album, dated May 1959 with the caption written in Mam's hand, 'Dee, sweltering May 1959'. And there I am, a two-year-old on a picnic rug, a little dress showing off my thin arms and thighs. There's a man's hand on the edge of the frame. Dad's? Maybe it was as warm as this, then. Even warmer.

We leave behind the kitchen garden with its neat drills of carrots, parsnips, beetroot, turnips and two rougher double drills of potatoes. The herb patch of parsley, mint and thyme is untidy. Tom Burke glowers over it. He tips his head in our direction but doesn't speak. Marge sets a spanking pace, jaw set, shoulders erect, the Olympic runner out for a refreshing few miles. Ahead of me, she seems even taller in shorts. I have to run to keep up. Cherry blossoms tickle our face on their way to ground. In another few days, their bright blooming will be over. We jump over the low stone wall to the orchard. One of the Harty children, Lally, I think, is swinging dreamily backwards and forwards while she reads a comic. The swing, a heavy wooden frame, is newly painted. Same colour as always, woodgreen. Greta and I spent hours quarrelling over who's turn it was to swing on it. Lally, the runt of the litter, doesn't even look our way. We pass through Horse field, not a horse in sight. Not back from their morning runs yet. Carduignan riding school has leased the field for grazing as long as I can remember. Bluebell field is just that. A mass of colour at this time of year. We run through the well worn paths, shrieking our delight. We sit on the Giant's Stone by the gateway. You can see the village from here. Just the one street. Post Office, church, school, Barry's petrol pumps, a scatter of houses, a mixture of converted cottages and new bungalows. At the farthest end of the village, just out of sight is the pottery and lace factory. Marge's husband, Tom, runs the business now. A cousin of Dad's, though he called him Uncle after he married Marge, he pulled it out of its decline through sheer hard work. Pender pottery and lace grace the best tables at home and abroad these days. Older than Marge by twenty years, they seem so well suited it's disconcerting.

'Disgusting is what I call it,' Greta said at the time of the engagement, 'robbing the cradle.'

'Forty-two isn't exactly old,' I protested.

'Not in your family perhaps, but Tom is the same age as Harty, old enough to be her father as far as I'm concerned. Your Mam and Dad are old enough to be your grandparents. Young to you is under fifty.'

And she was right of course. Tom was called 'Young Tom' in the family and it was difficult to think of him as a cradle snatcher. Equally difficult to think of Marge as a victim. At twenty-two, a business degree behind her, she knew what she wanted and that was that. No matter how many stones Greta cast her way, she brushed them off.

'Mixed marriages are always a risk, not to mention the age gap. You'll end up nursing him and waiting on him hand and foot. It's stupid to marry the first man that asks you. Is it your height that's worrying you? Okay, he's taller than you which is more than can be said for the runts of fellas in this parish, but there's thousands of tall men in Sweden or America. Don't do something in a hurry. You'll live to regret it.'

'I love him. I'd marry him if he was only five feet tall. We've known each other all our lives.'

All Greta's fears were foundless. Marge is in charge of export sales in the company and Tom and herself are very happy. Rachel and Simon are clever and energetic like their parents. As a family, they go mountain climbing, skiing, swimming, not to talk of tennis and riding. Their energy seems boundless. Tom at fifty-two is as fit as a man fifteen years his junior.

This must be a rare day off for Marge. Tom and herself work a six day week. On alternate Sundays, they go to Mass or the Church of Ireland service with the children.

The heat on the Giant's Stone seems intense. It's my hair. Not having it makes the difference. I feel the sun more. I ruffle my fingers through it and I'm newly shocked. 'Will we go to the village?' Marge asks.

'I don't think so, not today.'

'Just a crisp walk through, easier when you've done it once. You haven't been to the village in the last two weeks. It's not good to be cooped up. Two minutes will do it.'

'Thanks, but I want to get back.'

'For what?'

'I've telephone calls to make and letters to write to college, to the people taking over my classes. I must get it organised today.'

It's half true, but I really want to get back to the journal. I want to run my hands over its smooth brown cover. I'm ready for it. I can't bear to wait a second longer. I wish Marge would disappear.

'Are you sure? I'm not due in the pottery until after lunch.'

'Absolutely. I've taken up too much of your time already.'

She doesn't deny this.

'Race you home,' I dart down the side of the rock. She must have given me some kind of a head start because I don't see her for a while. I'm gasping at the herb patch when she dawdles to my side.

'That was a good sprint, Dee,' she says matter of factly.

I want to annihilate her regular breathing, her six foot of self assuredness but I smile weakly and say nothing because I'm breathless. Deirdre, Dee. Aunt Anne christened her children Marge and Sam, bold abbreviations from the start.

I look up and he's standing here. Right next to me at the herb patch.

'Hello, Sam,' Marge says, as if he'd just slipped out

from the house a few minutes ago. She moves forward and gives him a bear hug and kiss. My hands fly to my head, conscious anew of my plucked scalp.

'I came as soon as I could.'

'We weren't expecting you,' I squawk, a jangle of nerves.

'Hello, Dee,' and he puts his arms out. Those arms trigger a memory. I'm in bed, but not in my room. I'm in the blue room. I know this because the first thing I see is the cabinet of blue vases, one of Dad's many collections. Aunt Em and Aunt Alice are sitting either side of the fireplace on the pair of blue silk Lady chairs. Their fingers clack delicately, two more crocheted collars, I presume. The remains of a game of Scrabble lie on the crowded table. The clock with the Roman numerals chimes the half hour. They look up briefly and smile. Happy that time is passing as it should. There is a knock at the door.

'Come in,' they chorus, a command as well as an invitation.

It's Maureen. The girl from the village. Mrs Harty's 'left hand' as she calls her. She has a tea tray of blue china and she sets it down awkwardly. There is distant weeping from another room.

Maureen gawps, like me, in the direction of the sound. Aunt Em and Aunt Alice turn on the wireless. Dance music of sorts. Grown up music. There is an iced cake with six candles on it on the sideboard.

Greta, Marge and Sam come in with little packages. I sit up in bed, my face and arms all spots. Sam puts his arms out to hug me but the aunts chorus a forbidding 'no'. I am six years old. I have chicken pox.

'Jesus, you look a fright,' says Greta. 'Have you heard

about Larry? He did himself in.'

Adult Sam wears a beige suit. His pink face is prematurely lined from sun. He smiles from under a fringe of white-blonde hair. The green eyes seem deeper. He has little packages in his hands.

'Just a token,' he says as he gives them to us. A little elephant each. Carved to perfection. His beige suit matches Marge's khaki. I feel I'm in the way as they stand, heads together, examining her elephant.

'I'll tell Mrs Harty you're here,' I say.

'She knows. I've already feasted at her table.' He sounds formal, priggish. Then he laughs and the boy in short pants is here again.

'My hair.' I point to it in dumb show.

'It suits you.'

'Liar!' and I chase him round the herb patch. Tom Burke mutters his annoyance under his breath loud enough for me to hear.

* * *

I am in Mark's office chasing him round his desk. Our talk session is over. Even Ms Cordova, his secretary has gone home. It must be a Tuesday or Thursday . . . Anyway I'm chasing him.

Round and round the mulberry bush until we've run each other breathless. He's fitter than me but he pretends. We collapse on to the black leather couch. It's easy to imagine drowning on that couch. It pulls you down, down. I close my eyes.

After a while I get up slowly and stand over him. He keeps his eyes shut tight.

'Oh my!' I croon, 'we're all worn out with the sun.

Look at those burns. What can I do to make you comfortable? Only one thing for it. Calamine lotion, I'm afraid. No need to be afraid. Just keep still.'

I open the large bottle of body oil, pour it, then gently rub, rub, until he's covered in it. He groans with pleasure but he's not allowed to talk. Once he did. And I stopped immediately. The abrupt finish was too much for him. But that's only happened once. He knows what he likes. When he's oiled and aching, I mount him briskly. A quick heartless canter is what I need.

In his shower I scrub myself fiercely, a medical rub.

'You're really getting better,' he smiles, as he washes his oiled skin.

I see his hands shake and I know I am.

* * *

Tom and Marge sit at the top and bottom of the table. Sam and I face each other at either side. Rachel and Simon have gone to bed. French onion soup, roast lamb with carrots and courgettes, new potatoes, followed by trifle and cream, then coffee, cheese and crackers. Being with Sam has given me appetite. Tom cannot abide people being coy with food.

'A game of golf tomorrow?' Tom's voice has a tendency to boom. He looks at Sam.

'I haven't played for a while.'

'Do you good to blow away the cobwebs. Would four o'clock suit you?'

'I suppose so.'

'You should sleep most of tomorrow to catch up,' Marge says.

'I don't feel too bad. A bit disoriented, I suppose, but delighted to be here. I wish I had made the funeral though. The post is unpredictable and the phones have been on the blink for the last few weeks.'

'You don't have to be in Africa to have unpredictable post. I've boxes of stock held up in Dublin with this selective postal strike,' Tom says with unusual ferocity. 'Anyway, it's great to have you with us for a while.'

'Simon has set up your old train set in your room,' Marge says. 'He's dying to cross tracks with you.'

'I'll stay in 'Field End' for the first few days though, be company for Dee.'

'Yes, of course,' Marge says quickly but you can see she's disappointed.

'Splendid dinner, Marge,' he says, anxious to restore her good spirits.

'A great cook, your sister, the best,' Tom agrees.

'If you'd rather stay here with Marge, please do. I'm perfectly alright on my own,' I protest. Part of me means it. It would have been more peaceful to daydream about him. I won't be going back to New York for a while. I've written to Barry, Mark and my college. I scrawled a card to Greta saying, 'Sam's here. Will stay on a while. Will ring.' I ring her at her apartment and get some man with no English.

'Greeta, she no here. I new friend.' Why can't she put on her answering machine or get a man with English?

'Tell her Dee rang from Ireland.' I hang up. I've moved into the nursery. Abandoned my rosy bedroom and regressed further. It's right at the top. Slanted attic, double room. Small windows and even those are barred. Seems to suit me just now. Sam has helped me move Dad's desk from his study to here. It dominates the room, a large, dark oak monstrosity. I ride my rocking horse, Rockabye, as I read the journal.

I shouldn't need to write this but I do. My true nature is to hold things in, to let others take decisions, to stand on the sidelines. Sarah loves me in spite of this, though sometimes I'm sure it must weary her. I watch her head bend over those clever stitches of hers, just like I used to in the pattern room years ago. She can stitch and make and do. Such beautiful lace!
I collect. Beautiful things: vases, snuff boxes, watches, boxes, tiles, cameras, books, pictures, hip flasks. But I have made none of these. They became mine. Not because I made them. Years now since I've spun the wheel and made a pot. I cannot blame father anymore. He's long gone. True, he did damage, but my willpower could repair that. I chose this lethargy. Yet, I feel it's been thrust upon me. Alice and Em's energy diminishes mine. But that's fanciful. Merely a lazy excuse. Dee is a watcher too. Alert to disasters, maybe that's what holds her back. Sometimes she does not stutter. Is this when optimism and possibility rise? My father, Daniel, had a harsh tongue.
Wasn't it bad enough that you turned RC to marry her but you had to pick the only one of the family who couldn't breed as well.

Rock, rock, Rockabye. Thirty-two years old and I still like to rock. Backwards and forwards, its sturdy polished wood will not give way. Forwards and backwards. I face the windows. I can see out of all four of them in spite of the bars. Dad held me up at the centre window and said, 'Look, look out there, Dee. What do you see?'

I looked past the kitchen garden, Horse field and

Bluebell field. Nothing new.

'Look at Horse field.'

I do. Six or seven horses are grazing as usual. The riding school horses.

'The bay in the corner is yours. Happy birthday from your old dad. Of course, you won't be able to ride him straight away. You'll have to wait until Dr Caird gives the all clear on your spots.'

'What's he called?'

'Sandy.'

'It suits him because of the colour but maybe Socks would be funnier. He looks as if he's wearing black ankle socks. Thank you, Dad. I'll call him Sandysocks.'

I hug him and he looks pleased. He has a homely tweedy smell, a faint hint of pipe tobacco too. Aunt Em and Aunt Alice nag him to give up smoking but he smiles through their talk, a cloud of smoke obscuring the humour in his eyes. We stay at the window for a while. The riding school children collect their horses for a run. Someone is taking Sandysocks. It's Greta. She's not togged out in jodhpurs and jacket like Marge and Sam. She's wearing a pair of her brother's trousers, Billy's, I presume. They're tucked into wellington boots that look two sizes too big. She leads Sandysocks from the field just like all the other children with their horses. He follows her.

'Greta asked if she could look after him while you're still confined to the house. She'll take good care of him.'

I smile but jealousy stabs my throat.

'I'd ... I'd ...'

He waits. He says nothing. Just waits.

'I'd like a ride ... a ride on Rockabye.'

'That's my girl.'

We leave the window and he lifts me on to tall, tall, Rockabye. Sturdy dark wood. I hold his reins tightly and Dad pushes me.

'F-a-s-t, faster,' I shout.

Rockabye's hooves fly through the air. Greta is left far, far behind.

There is a loud knock on the door. Sam's head twists round it.

'Morning, Dee,' he shouts above the galloping hooves, 'thought I heard trotting.'

'It's the music,' I point to the tape recorder, but stay on Rockabye. I slow down, from gallop to trot to rock, rock, rock. Out of tune with the music.

'Good old Rockabye,' he shouts above the noise, 'still going strong, I see.'

'Yes. Fair weather or foul he'll trot and gallop.'

He moves to the barred windows. Their height reaches his crotch. He bends. A giant in a doll's house.

'Another great day,' he shouts. 'Would you like to go for a ride?'

The tape ends abruptly. We laugh. I see a smudge of grey at his temples. Didn't notice it in the bright sunlight yesterday.

'I don't think so. Anyway, you've got a date at the golf course with Tom.'

'That's not until the afternoon.'

'I don't want to be slotted into a schedule.' I'm suddenly tetchy. 'I don't want to be part of any list.'

'What list?'

'Marge and you always had lists. The days neatly divided up into meaningful activities. I suppose you thought of it as self improvement.'

'What are you talking about?'

'Visit Dee. She has chicken pox, read her two pages of *Alice in Wonderland*. I picked up the windfalls for Tom.'

I am rocking again, building speed.

'You were eight years old and I was six. Even then you worked to an agenda.'

The gorgeous upper lip is being pulled in, teeth marking tiny pains. He doesn't speak, just looks at his feet, then slowly his eyes connect again with Rockabye and me.

'Dee, you've changed. I've had nothing to go by except your letters. They're always cheerful. Just like the old Dee.'

'That was me alright,' I talk in time to the rocking rhythms, 'cheerful Dee, the old Dee, the never-rock-the-boat-Dee.'

I don't want to cry but that's what I'm doing. Rocking and shaking with tears.

The bell clangs from the kitchen.

'That woman has gone stark raving mad. Clanging and banging for breakfast, dinner and supper these days. People get a taste for things and then they can't give them up. Bells, chocolate, it's all the one.'

I jerk Rockabye to a standstill and dismount. I wash my face and hands in the tiny sink, drying them as roughly as I can.

'There, don't I look a treat! We mustn't keep Mrs Harty waiting,' and I'm out the door and heading down the stairs before I hear Sam's footsteps behind me.

One of my outbursts? That's what Barry would call it. A proud proclamation. Mark has helped me develop

Belonging

the ability to let go:

'Let it all out, Deirdre. Your head is like a pressure cooker. Years of keeping the lid on but you've been up to full pressure most of the time.'

Celtic temperament, Barry calls it.

I was delighted to see Sam but that was yesterday. Now, I think it was better missing him, imagining him far away, untouchable as always.

If Barry were here now, we could sneak off to the yellow room tonight, just like we did last summer. It would keep me going through the day. The yellow room. The one farthest from Mam's sewing room and Dad's study. They were frail then. But I'd always thought of them as frail. When Greta's gran died at sixty, she said, 'It isn't fair. Your Mam is older and she's no notion of dyin'. She's just a bloody creakin' door.' And it's true, Mam had always been 'delicate'. That's what Dad called it anyway. Now that I know what 'delicate' meant in her case, it seems insensitive not to have guessed.

And she never complained. I'll have to say that for her. Just lay down in her 'Sleeping Room,' the one off the sewing room. That's where she felt most comfortable. I'm passing it now, Sam politely two steps behind, not saying a word. A bed, a table for medicines and the wireless. The yellow and blue tiled fireplace and the green armchair. I knew I was never to go in there unless another adult brought me. Sometimes she'd be in there for days and I'd be brought in to visit. Other times she'd hardly be there at all except for a nap after a long session in the sewing room. I felt excluded. That's all. The nuns automatically included her in Prayers for the Sick at school. A few times when prayer time came round and one of them read out her name, I wanted to put up my hand and say that she was quite well today, thank you, but I never did.

Mam in bed in one of her many white linen nighties. Lace collars she'd made herself, hair still fair till the day she died, tied in two girlish plaits. An elderly child, surrounded by her pattern books, medicines and music. Always music from the radio. Never voices. She said to me once, 'There are too many words in the world and people use them so carelessly. Music is more intimate.'

Her hands were always busy when she had the strength. Maybe that's why mine felt empty somehow. The clothes she made for me. Beautiful. Too beautiful. A self-conscious child already, they made me doubly so. Marge looked perfect in the dresses Aunt Anne or even Mam made for her. She looked as if they'd grown on her. Greta, when my dresses were passed on to her, looked magical, an exotic wild princess. But on me, their elaboration exaggerated my slight frame, dragged me down. These days I go for plain cuts and fabrics. I won't have any truck with frills, layers or elaborate details. My feminist friends think this has something to do with my view of woman as fashion victim but to me such dresses smell of the sick room, the weight of false delight lodged in the neck like a stone.

'I . . . I . . . I . . .' Too often the voice trailed off in a trinity of failure.

I don't know whether my stutter or Mam's martyrdom stung me the most. Impossible to voice unease with the confections she stitched for me when they gave her such joy. I felt guilty, ungrateful and miserable: a combination of feelings which guaranteed continued discomfort. I went to the Giant's Stone to voice my misery. Standing on top of it and with a view of the village I cursed quietly to air and wind. The blasphemies whipped about my head without pause or stutter.

They got help for me. Tuesdays and Thursdays a Miss Bateman came to the house. Broadfaced and broadhipped, she seemed a giant. Hair in tight black curls that never moved even when she shook her head from side to side. Her body was encased in a navy suit. We had class in the drawing room, the heavy oak table, chairs and cabinets bearing silent witness to my many humiliations. I used to stare at a painting of a fat Madonna and Child above the piano and wish that I could be a silent infant once more.

Miss Bateman was thorough. Breathing exercises, vowel sounds and consonants were marched out for inspection and if I often tripped over them she hinted that this was merely a temporary untidy affair that could be mopped up with a little discipline. She would provide the discipline, of course.

She let me choke and gargle and splutter and said we were making progress, weren't we, just a matter of time. How much time I wondered? Forever it seemed, a lifetime of Tuesdays and Thursdays mapped out for me, endlessly repeating, 'I owe you a large sum of money' or 'Did you burn that bun, you naughty child?' I learned rhymes and singing too. It was the singing that cracked it in the end.

'Have you ever heard a singer stutter?' she boomed at me one day.

I thought for a moment, then shook my head.

'Speak,' she commanded, tapping the air with a short

baton.

'N-N-No,' I managed.

'Of course you haven't,' she confirmed my faltering agreement as if it had been aggressive contradiction. 'We will free your voice through song.'

And incredibly, she did. I learned songs that had little meaning for me but I sang them without faltering.

'Did You Not See My Lady Go Down The Garden Singing?' was one of them.

'When you feel a stammer coming on, sing.'

All very well if life is a musical, I thought. But I found, if I could imagine I was singing, that was enough to make the words come out smoothly.

'You are a pianist and now you are a singer. You will be able to accompany yourself as you sing. What a lucky girl! We'll give a concert.'

My throat froze on the word.

'About time. The breakfast is half burned. Didn't ye hear the bell?' says Mrs Harty, 'you'll be glad of some real food, Sam, after all that foreign rice.'

* * *

It's one thing to feel you don't belong: it's another being presented with proof that you do not. The journal. Its cover now imprinted with my sweat prints belongs in my palm. I rub it, warm its battered leather with my touch. Holding it comforts and disturbs. I do not feel complete without it. If I cannot hold it, for instance, when I am with others, I have to have it nearby. I put it in a bag, a drawer or sometimes in Mam's sewing basket. Inside the old leather cover, it is made up of old school copybooks, four of them. The cheaper type, rough paper, blue-lined. My copybooks, maybe. Extra ones were kept in the kitchen dresser. Dad wrote with his precise fountain pen in these copies. Quink ink. Always blue, never black. I can remember him filling his pen at his desk. Utter concentration and contentment at the same time. There is one copy written in black ink, in Hungarian, I think.

Last night I could not sleep. For a long time I stared into darkness. Now that my past isn't mine, it seems more distant from me, even more silent. At last I slept. In my dreams I wandered unfamiliar rooms. Large, airy but yet dusty from disuse. Empty. This surprised me. I said, 'How terrible to live in a house without stairs!' Then I woke up, the remains of a Knickerbocker Glory creaming my unwashed teeth, nausea rising.

Some people throw up easily, others do not. Greta can puke at will. I hang on to the best and worst things. Vomit and faeces, old dolls, tattered books. I cringed over the bathroom bowl and willed my stomach to yield the remnants of the night gorge but it would not.

Mam never vomited either, not even when she was very ill. She would sit up in her sick bed, propped by thick bolsters. She hated pillows. Her reading was confined to Catholic Truth Society pamphlets. Membership, one guinea a year. Apart from her sewing, reading about the tortured lives of the saints was her only form of escapism. St Gertrude was a favourite. Sick in her convent in Helfta most of her life and dead by 1302, though authorities differ as to dates, this woman glowed through Mam's illnesses. Stigmata, the Five Sacred Wounds printed on St Gertrude's heart, not garishly on the flesh as in Padre Pio. This maimed mystic sent my tongue lolloping in my teeth even after my speech lessons. Candles were lit to Gertrude on each 17 November. Mam would whisper in reverential whispers, 'Sweet Jesus, I thank Thee for all the benefits Thou didst bestow on thy virgin Gertrude, Thy beloved spouse.' Dad and I would mumble 'Amen.' Mrs Harty would cymbal the end of the observance with a clatter of teacups and a derisive snort, 'Foreign saints. Poor St Brigid doesn't get a look in these days.'

Greta loved the St Gertrude teas. She stuffed herself with huge slabs of chocolate cake made from the 'teas fit for princesses' in Mrs Harty's scrapbook. I matched her in greed.

Brushing my teeth helps remove the glutinous remains of my midnight confection. I sit on the loo hoping to evacuate from that end. Nothing doing. I wobble back to bed. A Lourdes Madonna (a gift to Mam from Mrs Harty) is greenly luminous on the chest of drawers. She smirks a sickly Ave. I hug an ancient teddy and squint at it. Open, close, open. Green patterns swirl, collide. I puke. Poor Teddy gets the worst of it. I lie when I say I cannot vomit. There was a time when I couldn't stop. But that was a brief period, though it seemed an eternity. Three months. I got through quite a lot of chocolate cake at that time too. My cravings seemed to have no limit. I remember streams of brown vomit swirling down sinks and loos and Greta and Barry begging me to change my mind. They went on their knees, a grotesque parody of appeal. If you've never vomited spontaneously in your life and then suddenly you can't rely on yourself not to spurt and spew, you know you're out of control, not in charge.

Several times I had to run from class, my hands cupped to my mouth, leaving my students without explanation. Barry and Greta came to the clinic with me. I didn't want them there but they insisted and I was too weak to protest. I wanted it to be over, that's all. Baby, baby, baby. Barry had researched Celtic names, reading them to me in bed — Fiacra, Ciara, Medbh — a litany of stones to beat me. Greta cajoled with assurances that motherhood was natural and one adjusted when the baby arrived.

'It's not as if you're a baby yourself. Thirty is just right to become a mother. If you don't do it now, when will you do it?'

I could see the logic in her point of view. I had financial security and a stable relationship. There was no obstacle really except the enormous one inside my head. I knew this baby would never arrive, knew I couldn't possibly let it.

'If you kill the baby, it will be murder. Give it any name you like but that's what it is no matter how you look at it.' The cold finality of her words locked me out. I twisted and turned in explanations. I said it all. Wrong time, fear of responsibility, the baby didn't deserve a mother who wouldn't be fully committed to it.

'Bullshit, if you run away from this it will stay with you for the rest of your life. This baby wants to be born now, not when you decide to make some space in your filofax.'

In the end I blocked her voice out. I watched her mouth make shapes but I wouldn't let her words reach me. The world was suddenly full of pregnant women: on the subway, in Frank's Deli. Not to mention my

'Women Writers of the Twentieth Century' class. I looked up from my lecture notes on Sylvia Plath one afternoon — we were examining the theme of death in her poems. I caught the eye of Chrissy. She's twenty-three years old but looks about twelve with that honey-gold skin that won't allow wrinkles track her brow until she's at least a pensioner. She's sitting there smiling like a placid Buddha, nine months and one week pregnant.

The baby's overdue but she doesn't want an induction. The doctors are giving her until the end of the week. She says the baby will arrive of its own accord before the medical profession can get their cold instruments on it. At this moment in time, I know I do not understand anything about her. Nobody wants her to have this baby. Not her parents, not her lover who's an ambitious graduate student and doesn't want responsibility. Yet she's sitting in my class examining the art of dying, nine months and one week pregnant. My gorge rises and I flee the room. I spray the institutional green tiles but most of it reaches the toilet bowl. Another brown stream, the remains of a Mississippi mud pie from Frank's Deli gorged that morning as soon as he opened — 7.00am. Those tiles in the faculty loos are the same sickly green as this smirking Madonna. I hold teddy closely. I don't want to spread the mess about. The smell is foul. I reach for the bedside lamp. The nursery jumps into garish relief. Rockabye stares blankly out the window. His inanimate Patrician profile disdains mess. My baby would be speaking and walking now. Maybe calling my name or holding a teddy as she slept. I knew from the beginning it was a girl. I called her Em. Just Em. I talk to her still. Greta is right about so many things.

Dad's desk dwarfs the room. It looks about ten miles long even though it's crowded with stuff: the journal of course, books, photo albums. The house is empty, so I can clump about as much as I like, except I don't. Sam hired a car and took off yesterday with an address book to visit old friends. He expects them to be in the same places as they were ten years before his flight into Africa. Knowing his kind of luck, they'll be there and what's more they'll be pleased to see him. I think he's disappointed in me but it works both ways. Claiming adoption by my parents and seeking my real ones has made him conclude I'm deranged. He puts the journal down to 'Uncle's literary frustrations'. I wasn't going to show it to him at all. In fact instinct warned me that I shouldn't, but he caught me unawares. It was three o'clock in the morning, the night before last, when I was raiding the fridge. I hadn't eaten all day. My plate was full. Cashel blue cheese on aisles of French bread, hazelnut yoghurt drowning fresh fruit salad, two Mars bars.

'I'm worried about you,' he said softly, so softly I had to lean forward to catch the words.

'No need to be,' I said as casually as I could, picking up my tray of goodies and heading for the door. I had just reached for the knob to pull the door open when his hand claimed my tray and he stood in front of the door. Suddenly, he was an impassable giant and I was a Lilliputian.

'I . . . I . . . I . . .' I stopped. I wanted to say, 'I'm fine, don't worry.' For some reason I was meticulously focusing on the smudge of grey hairs above his left ear, the ear pinkly vulnerable. I leaned forward tenderly and kissed it. He dropped the tray. Nothing but breakages and mess since I came. Culinary cacophonies!

We both went to retrieve the pieces and bumped our heads. He laughed. That wide smile. Then I could see the fair-haired boy in long short pants. The boy with the flaky summer torso of Calamine lotion. The boy I was always trying to separate from Marge. The boy I kissed in the cave. He kissed me this time. Not the cave kiss but suncracked dry lips. Their urgency hurt me. I pulled away but his arms held me in a tight circle.

'This is silly,' I said.

He didn't answer me. I felt cold even though the night was muggy after a day of baking heat. I had nothing on but a knee-length Snoopy T-shirt I had thought suitable night attire for the nursery. Normally I wear severe mannish pyjamas. Mark says I'm afraid of losing control and the pyjamas are a mere symptom. These random thoughts went through my head as I pushed Sam away from me.

'Stop,' I say.

He lets me go, a red blotch of embarrassment colours his neck, creeps to his face.

'I'll clean up the mess,' he points to the upturned tray on the floor. Then he bends to the task in silent concentration.

'Stay here until I come back,' I say as I run from the kitchen.

I go to Mam's sewing room and get her best cutting scissors. I pull off the T-shirt and start cutting. I want to cut it into tiny pieces but I've neither patience nor skill. I hack it into sections. I pick up Dad's journal from her sewing box and run back to the kitchen with it. He is pouring Ovaltine into mugs with casual serenity. I throw the remnants of the T-shirt at him. One piece lands on his head, Snoopy's ear.

I stand there naked reading out Dad's entry for March 1957.

The baby has arrived safely. An easy birth, though she weighs only 5 lbs. The arrangements for Canada can now go ahead. She is a strong minded young woman and should do well there. Her English improves every visit. She is learning quickly.

'That is about me,' I shove the journal under his nose. He recoils. The remnants of the T-shirt are on the floor and we both stare at them dully.

'It's not about you, Dee. It's the month you were born but the rest is a muddle.' As he says this, I see him examine my nakedness and he moves back further from me. He reaches for Mrs Harty's overall hanging on a hook on the door, offers it to me but I don't take it.

'It's fantasy, Uncle's hobby, that's all.'

His voice is schoolmasterly persuasive, something apart.

'You get upset and see things differently, that's all. Then you persuade yourself you're right about them. You've always had extreme reactions. Part of your charm but also dangerous. Remember Baylad?'

His question hangs between us. I'm tempted not to answer but change my mind.

'I loved Sandysocks. Baylad could never replace him.'

'Uncle spent money on another horse because he loved you. You punished him by rejecting Baylad. He never said anything of course. You're selfish and spoilt. You always were. When things don't go your way you retreat behind fantasy.'

'I suppose what happened here tonight just happened in my head, another fantasy,' but my voice shakes and lacks conviction.

I run from him and his Ovaltine which has already formed a skin. I need to wash. This house has no shower and I used up all the hot water earlier in a bath before bedtime. I fill the bath. It's cold water but it will have to do. I step in and kneel in it.

My skin has not changed colour. I scrub it harshly, the way I used to after a long run with Sandysocks. Then it was invigorating. When Sandysocks died I bathed myself three and four times a day. I couldn't get rid of the smell of burning flesh. His flesh. It seemed to me it had gotten under my skin. I was surprised that strangers didn't run away from me in the streets. It went on for months, the incessant washing. Eventually, Aunt Alice filled my pockets with scented lavender sachets and my bedroom too. She put them everywhere, in drawers, on my dressing table, even tied a necklace of them around Rockabye's neck. And it went.

Now, I want to wash my skin off altogether, replace it. I think of his pink ear but that seems a long time ago. Maybe I shouldn't have kissed it. I towel myself roughly and put on an old woollen dressing gown of Mam's. I am shivering uncontrollably now. The gown feels scratchy on the skin. I fill a sinkful of water and dunk my head in and out of it. My spiky ends are flattened. My hair sticks to my head. I return to the nursery. I could have a drink. The gin bottle smiles from Dad's desk but I know if I have one drink I'll want to finish the bottle. Like the time I came back to my apartment after the clinic.

When I checked out, they were waiting in the visitors' foyer. I didn't want them there. I just wanted to get a cab and go straight home to bed on my own. Barry was flicking through a magazine pretending to read it. Greta was sitting on a tubular steel chair giving great attention to a picture that was merely two blobs and a line. I thought of sneaking by them but that was impossible. You had to sign out and pick up your receipt at the desk. So I went to the receptionist and signed.

They sat either side of me in the cab. Barry held my hand loosely as if he felt he should. Greta tried to put an arm around me but I sat back against the seat to prevent her. She twiddled with the ends of my long hair, plaiting and unplaiting them. I was thinking about the time I played egg tricks on Dad when I was small. You know the trick, the empty upturned shell. He pretended it was terrific each time.

Well, I'd emptied my own eggs this time round. Cleaned out, drained. Being a mother was beyond me, territory to be kept at bay. An invasion I couldn't accept. Barry hummed a tune — a lament, its whine intermingling with the raucous traffic of the New York streets. The cab driver told him to 'button it, Mac,' and I was pleased. The eerie air called up universal tragedy.

* * *

They had to leave me in the apartment — Barry had to deliver a lecture on 'Lamentation and repetition in the folksongs of Stirkov' and Greta was in mid rehearsal with a dreadful play off Broadway called *Stirrups, Nature and Me*. So I killed the afternoon with a half bottle of gin and listened to Jacqueline du Près play Elgar's Cello Concerto over and over on the stereo. Finally, I crawled on to our high hard bed and cried for my baby. I must have dozed off because I woke to the sound of the phone.

I let the answering machine deal with it. After the bleeps Mark's phoney concern filled the room. 'Hello, Dee, this is Dr Mark Phibbs calling. I hope everything went well for you today. I'll see you next Thursday for your usual appointment but if you need to call me before then, please do.'

It was the 'please do' that got me. He'd picked it up on his last trip to England and made it his own. But it didn't sit naturally on his tongue and never would. Its very falseness irked me now. The calm restraint, the note of query. If that's all he could come up with after years of me spilling my innards, then it was pathetic. I would make up stories to tell Mark from now on. Watch while he tried to unravel them into meaning.

All through the nausea, the spontaneous vomiting, he had told me my life had become disorderly and confused because of my negative mother-complex. According to Mark, I abhorred the notion of childbirth because I wanted to be as unlike my mother as I possibly could. She spent her life between the sewing room and the sickroom. I spent my time developing my intellect and fighting my way through faculty meetings. Can he be right? I wondered that spring afternoon as I thought about my empty bleeding womb. I thought of Mam's sewing. Love that had stitched and pinned me to inhibition and wordlessness.

Was that my own awkwardness? My cast-offs spun Greta to fluidity and grace. They fitted, light as air. And she had words to spare. Her tongue never locked except when she wanted silence. I slept then, empty, envious, full of self pity. But it was a dreamless sleep. No witches stalked my dreams. No baby's fingers poked from cauldrons. I woke to Barry rubbing my hair. I could smell whiskey on his breath. There was music. Loud whirling notes, interspersed with soft elegiac strains. The apartment was full of it.

'Turn down the stereo,' I muttered and turned from him.

'It's Stirkov and Vladatsky,' he giggled.

'I know,' I said, 'I've been listening to your tape for weeks.'

'No, they're here. It's a live performance. Stirkov's girl is a real looker, smart too. That's her on the second fiddle.'

'What are they doing here?'

'We invited them months ago, to come to dinner after my lecture. Don't you remember?'

I remembered now. Of course I did. But so much had happened in between. And today of all days!

'They can't eat here. There's no food and I have to sleep,' I tumbled the words out, anger expelling air and snorts.

'It's alright, *a leanbh*, I got a takeaway from Frank's Deli.'

A leanbh! He'd been taking Irish language classes at the Institute two evenings a week but this was the first time I heard him say a word *as Gaeilge*.

'You're a total bastard,' I said. 'Don't you *a leanbh* me. How dare you!'

'Didn't I use it properly?' he said softly. 'I thought it was a term of endearment.'

What is this, a lesson in linguistics?

'Go away. Go back to your friends and keep the noise down. Tell them I'm sick.'

I pushed him from me and in the acquiescence that sometimes comes with drink, he stumbled through the now dark bedroom back to the living room, closing the door with exaggerated quietness behind him.

Leanbh, baby, child. I hugged the words to me, rocking back and forth.

'I feel a funeral in my brain . . .' I said out loud to the room. Then I fumbled about, not wanting to put on a light, until I located the bottle of gin and my glass. The tonic was in the living room and I didn't want to go there. I just sat up, filling and refilling my glass. Downing the stuff, compulsory medicine.

It's pointless raking over old ground, I think, as I wash the puke and the remnants of the disgorged Knickerbocker Glory from teddy. I fill the sink and immerse him. He is striking water with his pudgy limbs. I pull off the top of my pyjamas and run it under the cold tap in the bath. Half chewed cherries and gungy banana particles trap the plughole. Then I think, what other ground do I have to rake over? Maybe I should start at the beginning. My beginning. If my mother was Hungarian then I will explore my real origins. I will go back, because I want to, because I need to. I can't skulk here in the house in Cork much longer or I will lose the will to do anything at all. Except, maybe, resist Mrs Harty's cooking by day and gorge myself on infantile feasts by night. I will go to

Limerick. According to the newspaper cuttings in the third copy in Dad's journal there was a Hungarian refugee camp there in 1956-1957.

2

LIES, LIMERICK AND HUNGARY

I HIRE A CAR. A Mini. Mrs Harty is dismayed.

'You'll be killed stone dead in that tin box.'

That's her benediction of dismay as I pull out of the driveway. Marge tells her to 'shush' and holds her smile and hand in place until I'm out of sight. I have behaved myself for days in preparation for this jaunt. I told them I was visiting old college friends, just like Sam. People are always reassured if you tell them you're visiting friends. Truth is, I never made any friends as an undergraduate. Painfully shy and terrified of stammering, I was the student who never spoke, not even in tutorials. I made up friends to write home about at the time. There was Geraldine from Listowel and Tara from Macroom. I included them in letters to reassure Mam and Dad. They were as real to me as the writers who interested me, Emily Dickinson, Sylvia Plath. I got so used to Geraldine and Tara that I worried over their flus and essays just as much as my own. I talked to Sylvia and Emily too but those conversations had a higher tone. Love, death and destiny.

Marge and Mrs Harty hoped I'd enjoy seeing Tara and Geraldine again, now both by happy coincidence married in Limerick. Mrs Harty said I'd find the triplets a handful but I assured her that Geraldine had a wonderful *au pair*, Inga, and while we'd arranged to bring the triplets on one or two short outings, we'd agreed it would be too much for poor Tara to be faced with three gurgling infants every day since herself and Patrick were dying to have babies and couldn't. Furthermore, I assured Mrs Harty that I'd taken the precaution of booking a room in the George Hotel as Geraldine's house was bursting at the seams with pampers and toys. Tara's aunts, two elderly retired nurses from Seattle, were staying with her for a fortnight.

I needed a rest by the time I got to Cork city, never mind making it all the way to Limerick. And it wasn't only the driving either, although it took me quite a while to adjust to driving on the left side of the road. Even before I left the village I had a narrow escape. I nearly went smack into a van as I turned the corner after the pottery. Mick Haley was driving. A careful driver, Mick retires next year from the pottery and he wouldn't want me or anyone else to blot his record. I asked him not to mention it to Marge or Tom as it would only worry them. It felt like hours later by the time I turned into Grand Parade and pulled in to park in front of the library.

I was startled by the searing sunshine and put my sunglasses on again. Weakened, that's what I felt. Twenty miles only from the house to Cork city, but already I needed a break. The tension of the drive and the feeling of suppressed excitement at my escape and necessary deceptions had exhausted me. I needed some caffeine in my system before I went any further. I headed in the direction of the Imperial Hotel.

I've been in rooms before with people who didn't realise I had been in college with them. They look at you and smile as they realise you're familiar from somewhere but they can't remember. I leave them guessing but I always return the smile. Why break the silence barrier? But this was different.

When I sat down with my coffee, the blonde woman with the loud voice at the next table looked right at me. It was Bella Butcher. Extraordinary that someone could look so different and yet the same. The hair was blonder, the voice louder, the skin a hard brown. Sun-kissed, some would say, but there was a dry parched quality about it as if it might age suddenly before one's eyes.

'Deirdre, Dee, Dee Pender . . . it is you, isn't it?'

I had to admit it. There was no escape.

'I suppose so,' I said but Bella was always immune to irony.

'Of course it is,' she reassured me heartily, 'Jeremy, this is Dee, an old college friend. It's been ages,' she neighed.

Jeremy smiled.

'You've just come at the right time. Jeremy has been preaching thrift. You've really rescued me.'

Like I did once before, I thought. Coleridge. My essay on Coleridge. She stole it though I couldn't prove it. We had been in the same English tutorial group all the way through college but we hadn't spoken much. Like I said, I didn't become a talker until I went to live in America. I'm quite certain I never spoke to Bella until Greta's first wedding. She was a cousin of the groom. The reception was in the Imperial, by the way. But that was several years after the Coleridge incident.

It was summer term in our final year and I had lost my preparatory notes for my essay on Coleridge, or so I thought. At the next tutorial I couldn't believe my ears when I heard Bella read out her essay in ringing tones. It was, in effect, my notes strung into essay form. Her tale of Coleridge joining the 15th Light Dragoons as Trooper Silas Tomkyn Comerbache and having to be rescued by his brothers drew laughs all round.

'I'm not into rescuing anyone these days, Bella,' I say lightly, 'and I've lost all interest in Coleridge.'

'Coleridge?' Jeremy enquires.

'A college joke,' I reassure him. Curiously, settling an old score twelve years on isn't all pleasure but I'm glad I did it all the same. That shy tongue-tied girl on the edge of tutorials is happy for me.

'Dee is an intellectual. All her jokes are literary,' Bella says in swift recovery.

Brian, Bella's cousin and Greta's husband was a tall blond man with compelling energy and a mesmeric personality. At the time of the wedding he was making a fortune on voice-overs for a well-known brand of coffee, seducing viewers with his mellifluous tones into raising their caffeine intake by startling amounts. He had only two professional stage performances behind him, both juvenile romantic leads. Playing himself, in fact. Harty was against the marriage from the start on the grounds that acting wasn't a real job for a man and it wouldn't ensure a reliable income. Mrs Harty said love and nature would settle things in their own way, and so, Greta was beautifully done out in Pender lace for the wedding. At the reception, Greta coaxed Dad on to the dance floor and Mam waltzed with Harty.

Bella talked her way through the reception, entertaining everyone with chat and gossip and including me retrospectively in high jinks and events at college in which I had never participated. I smiled but didn't interrupt her. At that time I was still socially catatonic. Mam asked her about Geraldine and Tara. She said she didn't know them very well, as they hadn't been in the same tutorial group as us. The inclusive 'us' froze my innards but mouse that I was, I held my peace.

'How's Brian?' I ask.

'He hasn't a hair on his head at the moment. He shaved it all off to play a Buddhist monk in *Saffron and Silence*. It's getting great houses though, so he's quite pleased. And how's Greta?'

'She's fine as far as I know. I've been here for the past six weeks. My parents died.'

'That's right,' she gasps. 'Brian went to the funeral. Like two swans, dying so closely together.'

'They were close,' I affirm, wishing to put a stop to the conversation.

'The girls are coming over to Brian for August. He's really looking forward to that. I missed them the last time they came. Greta is doing a terrific job on them, I hear.'

It's easy to be a good parent for a month. It's the other eleven months in the year that are tough going. Every September, Róisín and Cáit come back from Ireland after a month of indulgences from Brian and it takes until Hallowe'en for Greta to settle them into an acceptable routine again. She has terrific patience with children.

Bella and Jeremy finish their coffee and she presses me to visit them in Midleton but I explain about my visit to Geraldine and Tara in Limerick. After Limerick, she suggests, and I nod a maybe. I lie and say I may have to go back to New York to teach summer school in August, though I've already made arrangements for Cathy Wolston to take my classes on Flannery O'Connor. We pump hands and smile and they're on their way.

I'm on familiar territory now, mooning over cups of coffee in Cork. I put on my sunglasses again just in case of the unlikely event that someone else will ambush me. My eye catches the headline on the newspaper which the man opposite me is reading. It says, HUNGARY: THOUSANDS FILE PAST IMRE NAGY'S COFFIN IN HEROES' SQUARE. News of Hungary seems to be all around me since I read Dad's journal, just as the world was crammed with pregnant women for three months last year. I followed the story avidly on last night's TV news. Imre Nagy, thirty-one years after he was executed as a traitor and tossed into an unmarked grave at the back of Ujkoztemo cemetery, has been dug up and given a state funeral. He is no longer a traitor. He is a hero. Can I dig up my past and uncover the bones of truth thirty-two years later? Surely that's the very reason Dad left the journal. I am over some of the anger now, or think I am. I have gorged it from my system with my infantile feasts. I have regurgitated the pieces. I am newly cleansed. Ready to excavate truth.

Mark says I chose to dedicate myself to feminist literature because it was the least valued when I was an undergraduate in Cork. I think I chose it because the writing excited me and I felt many writers were genuinely overlooked. He says I'm a puritan at heart and like to walk uphill. In a curious way Dad's journal makes sense of my early silences and stutters. My sense of unease was genuine.

I had only ever been to Limerick once before, on a shopping spree with Greta years ago. Mrs Harty took us. A day trip by bus to celebrate our Inter Cert results. We came home with bags of clothes from Todds and Roches Stores. We had dinner at the George Hotel: roast lamb, potatoes and carrots. The soup was tinned, Mrs Harty complained, but the apple tart was freshly baked. We sneaked into a café in the afternoon and had fish and chips and she was amazed when we had only a scone for supper that night.

'The dinner wasn't that good,' she sniffed, offended.

Poor Mam was sick when we returned. Just a headache, she said but her colour was bad.

'Rags, colourful cheap rags, that's what they've spent their money on, Mrs Pender,' Mrs Harty said, warming to her subject.

'Young people like to feel in fashion,' Mam said.

'Not a decent skirt between the pair of them,' Mrs Harty continued, 'I had to let them off in the end or I wouldn't have got a tap done for myself.'

'We had a great day of it, Ma, and you enjoyed yourself too. Admit it,' Greta said.

She was bobbing up and down pulling lurid T-shirts over her head one after the other until she resembled a loud onion.

The drive to Limerick has a few scary moments but I make it okay, park the car and register in the George. I take a shower. It's still very warm. There's a lazy feeling in the early evening and I lie down for a short nap before dinner. I wake to darkness. It's twelve o'clock. I had no idea I was that tired. For a moment I think about ringing Tara or Geraldine. Even at this late hour I figure they might like to hear from me. Only then do I realise that of course they're not here. I am afraid. I am lonely.

Much later I ring room service for coffee and a sandwich. When it comes I realise I'm not hungry and can't eat it but I gulp down the coffee thirstily. I sit up the rest of the night and study the book of photographs I found in Dad's study.

It is a small book with a few photos in black and white. They are by a photographer called Karoly Escher. One is of a man called 'Professor Piccard, 1930s'. He looks quite comical in a winter overcoat, hat and scarf. The eyes dance with humour behind little round glasses and his moustache covers his upper lip. Another picture is called 'Blind Musician'. A man, eyes closed, mouth agape with stumps of teeth saws away at a violin. His hair is cropped tightly. I can see only one ear, his left one. The final picture is called 'The Horse of the Apocalypse, 1937'. In this one, a man with a generous moustache, dressed formally in a three piece suit, holds the reins of a horse as he walks beside him on a beach. Little clouds of sand are kicked up. Clouds bank cumulously in the background. These are small photos in a small book. They look as if they were fitted together as a home-made book. There is no writing apart from the title on the book, 'Pictures from Hungary'.

I tell the same story at the three local newspapers. I am researching an article on the Hungarian Revolution in 1956. I am interested in the refugees who came to Limerick from Hungary at the time. I want to find out where some of them went after Limerick. The article is spanning thirty-three years, 1956-1989. Hungary is changing so quickly, almost each week, I gush. It will be published in America, I assure them. Yes, of course I'll send copies. I am presented with the yellowed newspapers of winter 1956 and spring 1957. The headlines are both pathetic and exciting.

I head for the camp at Knocklasheelin. An army camp. A refugee camp. Temporary dwellings then. Only one long low prefabricated building now. But it's not muddy or cold as it was in the newspaper accounts that December and the following spring. Unreal heat cracks the paint and reveals its life of wear and tear. I peer through windows. Part of the building seems to be used as an office. My newspaper research in Limerick matches Dad's cuttings in the copybook.

'Inga, Inga, Inga.' I shout her name to sky and trees. The entry in Dad's journal reads:

Inga is both foolish and courageous. She has lied about her age. Told them she was twenty-one instead of fifteen. Poor child! She thinks twenty-one is a wise age. I worry about her and this hunger strike business. The refugees are on hunger strike because they say there is no work or future for them in Limerick. They want to go to America or Canada. Days now and she has not eaten. She has a small statue of St Gertrude. She keeps it in the pocket of her skirt.

She will call the child Gertrude if it is a girl, Janos, after its father if a boy. The nuns have appealed to her to eat for the sake of the child. She is stubborn. The bishop visits the camp and brings assurances of passports for Canada and America. The strike is over.

I think of Inga, child-mother, my mother walking over Sarsfield bridge in Limerick, listening to seagulls squawk, holding me tight to her heart, thinking that twenty-one was wise. To go on hunger strike is an act of will. Asserting one's will through denial of food. To go on hunger strike when you are pregnant is both foolhardy and courageous. To have such will in a foreign country, remote from everything you have known is heroic. I applaud Inga. I think of Simone Weill in Middlesex hospital refusing food, not to take more than the rations of her compatriots in wartime France. Refusing food in England, then refusing to eat anything at all. Going out on an act of will. Becoming absolutely herself in spite of everyone around her. Inga, Simone, Simone, Inga. I have found a mother indeed. Not Mam, the pale invalid. On the prayer list for the sick all my life. Pulling me to her heart by anxious threads. But Inga who knew what she wanted and took what she could.

Inga Kadar went to Canada in May 1957. It says so on the list, the list in the newspaper office. She went to Toronto. There is no other Inga on the list. She came from Budapest. That's what it says. Inga Kadar from Budapest, refugee, stayed in Knocklasheelin Camp from December 1956 to May 1957. I will not follow her there. She did not intend that. But I will set my eyes towards Budapest.

* * *

Budapest. I get here by more lies. Mrs Harty and Marge think I'm in London with Tara and Geraldine. A shopping spree. They understand. They're relieved that

I'm doing normal things and with friends too. I come to London anyway and fly on to Budapest. Malev Airlines. It seems to be the national airline. Now that I'm in Hungary I realise I should have read more. Some history, maybe the language. The language sounds rough and unfriendly. I have a tourist dictionary. I practised some phrases on the plane journey with help from a fellow passenger, Lisa, an American, a journalist based in Budapest. She drills me in the basic phrases of the language during the flight.

The formal hello is 'jo napot, kivanok.' The informal hello is 'szervusz' and a casual hello is 'szia' (pronounced seeya) but on no account to be used when speaking to elderly people. The really confusing thing is that goodbye in Hungarian is 'halo'.

She tells me about a friend of hers, Ann. She's a terrific folkdancer and she came on a holiday to Budapest to dance with the natives. Except she can't find any folkdancers to dance with. Apparently the only way to get into a folkdancing group until recently was to join the local communist youth league. Lisa said that Ann trembled at the very word communism. Even the public portraits of Lenin upset her. In fact she was having a miserable time. Not a linguist, not even an amateur one, she couldn't get her tongue around the simplest phrases necessary for basic survival. The poor woman spent the first week starving as she pointed to produce in shops. She lost her nerve after countless wrong purchases.

We're drinking palinka, Lisa and I. It's a white drink, a bit like vodka but with a fruity taste. Lisa takes me under her wing. She knows Budapest well. Central and Eastern Europe is her territory. She's booked into the

Hilton, the usual monstrosity except that it had to incorporate some old monastic ruins into the courtyard as the authorities wouldn't allow the builders to knock it. She laughs when I'm startled by the appearance of the hotel.

'It's not as bad as Leningrad style,' she jokes. 'Blocks and blocks of housing projects, ten floors high, all square, early sixties utility. They call them lakotelep.'

'I think I saw some on the way from the airport.'

'Too right, you did. They're everywhere. Blocks and blocks of them.'

'But there are farms?'

'Sure, in the countryside. Some people tend to romanticise the little old farmhouses, the golden age of nostalgia and all that rubbish. The farming folk who lived in tanyas had it pretty rough. No electricity or water. Still, if you want to be romantic about it, you can visit entire villages that have been preserved. Holloko is one of them.'

I book into the Hilton too and then she takes me to the Gellert Hotel. An old hotel complete with marble and Turkish baths. Hot springs, cold springs. I'm a bit inhibited when I realise you're not allowed to wear anything in the springs but feel wonderful when the initial strain and fatigue of the journey is washed away. Lisa says that these baths are too expensive for most Hungarians. They have to go to public baths. I meet a seventy-five year old English woman, Freda, who comes here on holiday every year just for the baths. She claims they've almost cured her arthritis.

'You should try the public baths at Szechenyi,' she urges me, 'You can even play chess there in the water. They have floating sets made of cork. Basil and I have such fun. Quite a few Germans go there and they can be rather serious about their game. Basil and I were reprimanded by a German couple yesterday. My fault really, I couldn't stop giggling.'

Lisa and I are meeting Ann in Vorosmarty Square. This is on the Pest side of the Danube. We have coffee and cakes at the Gerbeaud Café. The dobostorte, pastry in layers, topped with chocolate and orange, is wonderful. People salute Lisa all the time. Mostly men. Short men, tall men, dark men, blond men. I had expected all Hungarians to be short, chunky and blackhaired but they're not. I say this to Lisa.

'There's no such thing as a Hungarian people. They arrived here in 900. They're as mixed as anyone else. Go towards Transylvania, and you'll see a tall blondish type. Ann is the expert on Transylvanians.'

'Just because I had dinner twice with two of them!' Ann is exclaiming in childish protest.

'They were gorgeous. Both of them,' Lisa teases, 'from their blond heads to their chiselled chins and who knows what other delights. But she threw them over. No stamina.'

'They couldn't dance,' Ann turns to me.

'In the dark?' Lisa persists, 'oh well, then they must have been unsuitable.'

'One of them killed himself,' Ann confides in me.

'Not because of the dancing,' Lisa nods assurance in my direction.

'But why?'

Ann is silent and makes no effort at an explanation.

'Hungary has the highest suicide rate in Europe,' Lisa says as she skewers another piece of pastry with her fork.

'Nobody knows who they are, so they kill themselves to find out, but then it is too late,' she laughs. I realise that I've come in such a rush that I know very little about where I am. Phrases like 'Austro-Hungarian Empire' and 'Russian occupation' echo from the back of the brain. Lessons half-learned in school long ago. I do not know if Lisa is playing with me or if what she says is true.

'Oh yes,' she sips her coffee with relish and orders another dobostorte, 'when I came here first I couldn't get used to having a drink with someone one evening and being told he had hung himself in his kitchen later that night. A feat indeed and incredibly selfish. Most families live in two rooms, so the bastard would have had to step over his sleeping wife and children to get to the pokey kitchen to accomplish the lousy deed. Nothing clean like downing tablets and going to sleep forever. They're an emotional lot, these Hungarians, and vengeful too.'

'Vengeful?'

'Yea, they have more reasons than most not to forget wrongs done to them. This is a crazy country, full of contradictions.'

'It's not only countries that are full of contradictions. Most people are too,' I add my tuppence worth.

Lisa's eyes narrow in suspicion.

'I hope you're not into pop psychology. That kind of stuff bores me rigid. I once dated a guy who had a whole shelf of *How To* books, *How to be successful*, *How to get fit in a week*, *How to handle stress*. All that crap. I didn't find out about the books until I visited his apartment on maybe our fifth date. He seemed interesting up until then but when I got an eyeful of his how to section, I bowed out.'

'I'm not into pop psychology but I like to have some understanding of human behaviour.'

'Understanding is overrated. Most people make a mess of it when they try to understand. I speak from experience.'

'But journalists need a high level of human psychology, surely, in their profession?'

'Not of people, only events. I was interviewing two old men recently for the paper. One was a retired MP. He'd started out as an onion merchant. Had no interest in politics. He brought his onions to market one day as usual. This was after the war. The Russian Commandant of the town surrounded the marketplace with his troops, put people into lorries and transported them to the provisional capital. When they got there, they were told they were now MPs. The other old man had been from a noble family. After the war, he was stripped of his property and belongings and sent into the countryside to work as a farm labourer, but not before they took all of his clothes. Those men lived it. What's there to understand?'

'There's a flaw in your logic but I'm not sure what it is. That happened in the forties and yet I bet they will remember it all of their lives. Maybe that's your flaw. They re-make it and make sense of it through memory. That's their way of understanding it.'

'They remember every minute of it as if it was only yesterday. True enough, at least they gave me a story. It's still difficult to get those involved in the 1956 rebellion to talk.'

'Some of them came to Ireland as refugees.'

'No kidding! I didn't know that.'

'Yes. We had national collections of money and clothes for them and even offers of adoption of Hungarian children.'

'A lot of people got out pretty fast after Imre Nagy told Andropov to hump the Warsaw pact. The Russians even fired on hospitals and ambulances after that.' Ann is impatient.

'I hate political talk,' she pouts.

She's a round roly-poly woman. The most unlikely dancer ever. Except maybe as one of those series of rounded Russian dolls that fit into each other. Difficult to judge her age. She could be anything from late twenties to late thirties. A wide round face, blue eyes topped with sheaves of corn-blonde hair. She's short and wears a curious blend of colours and patterns — a cross between old hippie and new ethnic.

'I'm heading back to Oregon one of these days. I've had enough of Hungarian hospitality.' Ann sounds as if she's trying to convince herself, not us.

The voice is childlike and intense, with something of the sing-song about it. Lisa counters this with stoicism.

'I told you it would take discipline to live in Hungary and you wouldn't believe me. You mustn't cry if the shopkeepers scream at you. They try that with everyone. And you have to have a few words of the language. They're not used to glastnost and perestroika yet. They still hate the Russians.'

'They're letting the Russians know what they really feel about them now. They cut the hammer, the cornsheaf and red star out of the national flag at the service for Imre Nagy. I was there in Heroes' Square.' Ann is excited.

'You hate the Russians too,' Lisa says.

'I only came for the folk dancing,' Lisa protests.

'And the Russians only came to protect freedom, in the first place. At least that's their story. I don't see why you couldn't have signed up with the Communist Youth League and danced with them a few nights a week. At least you would have accomplished something. Anyway, not to worry, the way things are moving these days you'll be able to start your own private folk dancing club and make it a proper tourist attraction.'

'I couldn't become a party member. Daddy would have a fit.'

'Her father's in the US army,' Lisa explains.

'I came to find my roots.' The cliché is out before I realise it.

'I thought Americans went to Ireland to find their roots. Irish women coming to Hungary to find theirs is new to me.' Lisa's abrupt observation stings.

'My . . . my parents may have been . . . Hung . . . ggg . . . arian.'

Ann is embarrassed. Lisa isn't.

'You said you were Irish on the plane and I can't help noticing you don't have any Hungarian.'

The barb is light, playful.

'Stop interrogating. She does this all the time.' Ann smiles at me.

'I'm interested in people. I like to get to the bottom of things. I'm a journalist, for Christ's sake. Curiosity is my middle name.'

'It's complicated,' I say.

'We all like to feel that about our lives. It makes us feel interesting. But usually lives are a simple affair.'

Her eyes fix me and I look into my coffee cup and

push my pastry around my plate. I'm suddenly aware of all the noisy voices around me. Most of them are gabbling in words I can't unravel. I want to leave. Go back to my hotel room. Pretend I'm a real tourist. But I'm not. I'm in London with Tara and Geraldine. I'm in Budapest with Lisa and Ann. I'm Deirdre, I'm Gertrude. I'm frightened.

'We even let East Germans escape into Austria these days. You've come at the best of times and the worst of times. The forint has been devalued twice in the last year. Change is in the air. It's a good time to be here, whatever your reasons. Hungary's on the road to democracy.'

'My mother may be in Canada. My father may be here.'

'You see, I told you. Lives are straightforward. Let's have dinner tonight. I'll pick you up and show you Buda by night. Now I really must leave you tourists and check in at the office. I'm working on a scintillating article on the Ozd steelworks.'

Later, Lisa and I eat dinner in a restaurant overlooking the city. The outside of the restaurant is painted pink and the walls, curtains, and linen of the interior are various shades of light pink. The atmosphere is warm. We have a window seat. The city, the Danube and its bridges are lit below us.

'This is the castle area,' Lisa instructs between spoonfuls of soup, 'Bela IV built the first castle here in the thirteenth century.'

I'm tired. I went with Ann earlier to one of the Folkart Centrums in the city. Ann bought a basketful of goods. She was disappointed I wasn't similarly enthused, so I bought a tablecloth.

'I didn't realise there were so many bridges in Budapest,' I observe to Lisa now.

'Rebuilt by slave labour after the war. They just collected people on the streets and told them to start building.'

I have cold apple soup (hideg amaleves) and chicken paprika (Csirke paprikas). It is good. The waiters are attentive. I feel guilty enjoying the food as I think of the forced labour that rebuilt the city.

'The vegetables are tinned,' Lisa says but I don't let that spoil my enjoyment. A lone violinist plays Mendelssohn on a little podium at the end of the dining room.

Lisa is talking but I'm only half listening. Then her tone changes and she has my full attention once more.

'So, spill the beans,' she says, 'your story, what you've come to find out,' her soup spoon is halfway to her mouth. She holds it there.

The restaurant is full. Three massive chandeliers light the room, casting soft shades on the miles of pink linen on each table. For some reason I want to fix these details in my head.

'Come, come, don't be coy,' she splashes her spoon back into the soup impatiently.

Part of me wants to talk and another part of me wants to conceal. I'm not used to talking about myself except to Mark and I've been telling him fairy tales for a long time. Greta knows me best and she agrees with Barry about this Hungarian business. She says I'm a right eejit to be chasing cock and bull stories. She says she'll sort me out in August when she comes with her daughters, Róisín and Cáit. Even she thinks I'm in London. There was something awkward about my last phonecall to Greta before I left. I couldn't figure out what it was but it stopped me confiding in her about this trip to Budapest. Maybe talking to Lisa, a complete stranger, could sort out some of my confusion. I take a deep breath and I start. I keep it simple, the bare bones.

'I am thirty-two years old. I teach in a college in New York. Literature. I was born in Ireland. I grew up in a small village in West Cork. The people whom I took to be my parents died the end of May this year, within a day of each other. Dad was eighty-two and Mam was seventy-seven. They were kind people and I loved them.

'I was a quiet inward child. My best friend Greta wasn't. I wanted to be like Greta when I was a child. She could sing and dance and act. She never stuttered. I went to America because Greta was living there and also I could study feminist literature at post-graduate level. I live with Barry. He's a musicologist and folklorist. He loves me because I am Irish.

'I talk to Mark, my shrink, twice a week but I've been telling him lies for a long time now. Dad left a journal with his solicitor when he died. It's confusing but it seems to imply that my mother was Hungarian. She came to Ireland as a refugee in the winter of 1956.

'The journal is made up of several copybooks. One short one is in Hungarian, I think. My cousins, Marge and Sam think that the journal is the beginnings of a novel. Greta agrees. They don't know I'm here. They think I'm in London with friends.'

Lisa does not speak. The violinist's music fills the space between us. I am staring at my chicken. I do not want to pick up my knife and fork and cut into it. My appetite has vanished. I don't want to eat a dead animal.

'You were right to come,' she says finally.

Lisa asks practical questions. She's curious about my birth cert.

It lists my parents as Sarah Louise O'Brien Pender and John Samuel Pender, I tell her. But then that could be easily fixed, I say, as old Dr Caird had been the Pender family doctor for decades. Unlikely but a possibility, she concedes. She can get a translator to look at the Hungarian copybook. I'm not sure I'm ready to surrender it just yet.

'Why are you so ready to believe you're not your parents' child? You'll probably find out there's a perfectly rational reason behind your father's journal. If anyone tried to decode my working notebooks, I'm sure I would be confined to a protected environment.'

'I felt uncomfortable during most of my childhood.'

'Most children do, more than parents realise. I had a bad run at one stage, must have lasted about five years I guess, whem I just couldn't tolerate my parents offering me any advice no matter how trivial. We had the most outrageous shouting matches.'

'There were silences in our house. They seemed to go on forever. It became difficult to break those silences. I considered what I might say but rarely said it.'

'You realise all of this has probably a very straightforward explanation. Maybe you were just shy and inhibited and they were thoughtful, quiet people. People talk too much nowadays. I know I do. Also, bereavement needs to be worked through. When my mom died I bought her birthday gifts for three years afterwards. Kept forgetting she was gone. A denial of death, I suppose. I felt physically exhausted for a long time.'

'Strange but I feel energised by these complications. My mother was an invalid for as long as I can remember. I think I felt guilty, responsible for her delicate state. Afraid to upset her in any way. This new mother, Inga, she's strong, she took chances. There's been very little room for chance in my life.'

'We all feel that at one time or another.'

'But you're a journalist. You take chances every day. You're only as good as your last article. That's really putting yourself on the line.'

'Sure,' her mild agreement leaves something in mid-air. We finish our meal and get a taxi back to the Hilton. I'm unable to sleep. Excitement and indecision crowd my head. I count sheep but concentrate too precisely on the numbers. My head is a jumble of random thoughts. How strange to have spent my last decade in New York and now to feel so remote from it. I imagine Barry in the Spring Street apartment tinkling a tune on the baby grand or tuning one of his many fiddles. Or I see him sprawled across our oak bed with the orthopaedic mattress. Both of us have bad backs. He reaches for me but I'm not there. I miss him. Miss his rituals, both in and out of bed. At least once a week he makes home-made bread and soup. Usually on Friday evenings, to signal the weekend. After that we usually eat in a Chinese or Indian restaurant two blocks away. Sometimes we take in an art opening in Soho or a late movie. Movies always make me randy. It doesn't matter what show is on, the effect is the same. I remember the first movie I saw. I called them films back then. It was *Mister Roberts*. Henry Fonda and James Cagney were in it. It was on in the Capitol cinema in Cork. Mrs Harty had a crush on Henry Fonda. She took myself and Greta to see it. I can't remember a thing about the plot but the excitement of being part of the world of films was wonderful. It was shortly after Greta's Gran died. I remember that because at the interval when all three of us were licking enormous ice cream cones, Mrs Harty said,

'Poor Gran, if she was here now, Greta, she'd be sendin' you out to the shop for her Afton Major.'

And myself and Greta piped up in unison,

'A hundred per cent Virginia leaf goes into them,' because that's what her Gran said every time she sent Greta for cigarettes.

And Harty would say, 'Some people must have money to burn, two and seven pence for twenty cigarettes.'

And Greta's Gran would say, 'How's your back, Harty?'

Zöe Peterson smokes very strong cigarettes too. I don't know if they're as strong as Afton Majors were. I know very few people who smoke these days. Zöe is one of my graduate students, smart and beautiful in the way tall Swedes are. Anyway, Irina, my Head of Department assured me in her last letter that Zöe is as industrious as ever. She has finished her paper on the Brontë sisters. She spent her last vacation in Haworth in Yorkshire. It rained all the time. She was amazed that the Brontës could be so creative in such damp isolation. I turn my mind to Dad's journal once more and decide to get a copy made and give it to Lisa. Time to take a chance. I fall asleep on this resolution.

As it turns out I didn't see Lisa for a few days. I find a note under my door next morning.

'Got to be in Szeged for two days. Explore the city. See you when I get back.'

And I do. Explore the city, I mean, but only in random fashion. I wander from place to place on foot or by taxi. I'm not ready yet to brave trams or subways. I stare at winged altars and Gothic woodcuts in the National Gallery and admire contemporary furniture at the Museum of Hungarian Workers. I have coffee at the Astoria and watch myself smiling into a mirror under an elaborate chandelier. I'm astonished at the daylong queues outside the Adidas shop in Vatci Utca. I buy a jug of spun glass at the Russian shop across from the Astoria. It's deep blue with swirls of green circling the base. Dad would have loved it. I thought of him the other day as well when I came across a very beautiful glass cup in the National Museum. Fourth century, early Christian.

'I love glass. Some glass, you can see through, other glass you can't. Just like people,' he said, last summer holidays when I helped him rearrange his Victorian bottle collection.

Ann accompanies me on the train to St Entendre, an artistic settlement on hilly terrain a short distance from the city. We wander through pottery and craft shops, visit a Siberian church. I buy some shirts from a group of Transylvanian women selling their wares on the streets. Beautiful stitchwork but not as lovely as Mam's. We finish the day's outing with dinner in an over-priced bijou French restaurant.

When Lisa returns I give her a copy of the Hungarian section of the journal.

'It may take some time,' she warns. 'The translator I use is very busy at the moment, but she's good.'

'Okay,' but as I hand it over I have last minute doubts.

The weather is muggy as the temperature goes up. I find I am a regular at the Gellert Baths, if one can become a regular within a week. Inhibitions gone, I revel in the water and feel relaxed.

'Now, for a different view of Budapest, I have arranged a little outing,' Lisa says during my second week, 'I wrote an article on this place recently. It was a concentration camp during the war. It's long before the 1956 revolution but it may be of interest to you.'

Next day we travel towards the Cjeck border. To Recsk. Two hours drive from Budapest, Lisa says but I'm not watching the time. Mountainous terrain. The roads wind and wind. Ann is in the back seat. She has not yet left for Oregon. Lisa's car holds the road but we have the excitement of two narrow escapes with Traubads, the car that Hungarians drive because they can't afford Ladas. We scrape by two of these in quick succession coming around bends.

Then we're there. Lisa stops the car. Pine forests. We are right in the middle of a forest. She points. 'Tessek,' she says simply.

She has used that word quite regularly over the past few days. I have grown used to it. It can mean any number of things. I have even grown bold and used it myself. It can mean, help yourself, come in, please, all of these things.

Political prisoners slaved here, carrying rocks from the quarry nearby. Now there's just a few blocks of concrete. She took me to a lakotelep yesterday. A housing project outside the city. Tall. Ten storeys high. Ugly square concrete box. No trees to shade ugliness.

Nothing near it to curve its harsh squareness. We climbed the smelly communal stairs. The door was answered immediately we knocked.

'Szervus,' the woman smiled, her mouth full of grey shiny fillings. Her hair was hidden under a black scarf. The room we stepped into was crammed full of people. A white-haired woman was in bed and the others stood around her. A grey-haired man in a string vest and baggy trousers took her hand and raised her almost in a dancelike movement from the bed. Two other men in matching brown suits in an instant turned the bed into a table. It was so fast my eyes didn't register the various stages. A young girl with plaited hair put a tablecloth on the table. The woman who let us in handed everyone in the room fold-up chairs. We adjusted them and sat down. The old woman put an apron on over her nightdress and went into the tiny kitchen which adjoined the room.

'Langos,' she said, 'langos,' she repeated and everyone nodded and smiled. Then they turned their attention to me.

'This is Judit,' Lisa said. The toothsome woman smiled.

'And this,' continued Lisa, pointing to each of the men in turn 'is Janos, Janos and Janos.'

'Jo napot, kivanok,' they said, a triumvirate of voices.

I nodded. One of them got glasses and another poured palinka. We drank. Very fast. Maybe four glasses, maybe five. My head began to swim.

'Jzesus Maria!' the grandmother swore at regular intervals.

There was a lot of talk. I could identify no meaning though beyond 'igem' (yes) and 'nem' (no).

'Langos,' the grandmother shouted loudly, 'Gertrude,' she called the young girl. The girl brought plates to her and she filled them. Then she placed them on the table in front of us. There were two pieces of hot yeastlike dough on my plate, puffed up and topped with cheese and garlic. I ate them greedily.

'Salad Kaposta,' the grandmother shouted next. Our plates were filled with sweet, and, sour shredded white cabbage, onion and pickles.

She smiled encouragement to us from the tiny kitchen and kept dishing out the food until the pot was empty. Then she joined us though she did not eat. She pulled out another one of the fold-up chairs and sat next to me, our knees bumping together, there was so little space.

I am thinking of those kind people as I stand here in the middle of the pine forest staring at a few blocks of concrete. Five of their extended family served time here. I asked about the young girl who handed around the plates of food. Gertrude. Another favourite family name. Janos and Kadar for boys. Judit and Gertrude for girls.

I who am Deirdre may have been Gertrude. A man called Janos may have been my father. Janus, the god, looked to the past and the future. He faced both ways. God of all beginnings: the year, the month, the day. That's what Sister Agnes used to say. A haze of heat hangs over these pine forests. The temperature is in the eighties today. I feel my cotton dress stick to me. A drink wouldn't go astray. How many of the prisoners who laboured here longed for a drink to break the monotony of their toil?

My thoughts are interrupted by music. Violin music

cuts the air. A familiar tune from where? From the apartment on Spring Street. Lisa is playing a violin. Ann is dancing. I did not know that Lisa could play. I didn't really believe that Ann could dance. Her movements are quick yet graceful. Hands and feet take movement from the forest air. Lisa spins the tune then slows to an ending. Ann stops with her. I clap.

'Bull's blood,' Ann shouts, 'nothing like a bottle of Hungarian red wine to raise the spirits.'

She goes to the car and gets bottle and glasses. 'A toast. To Janos and all those who passed through here,' Lisa raises her glass and we follow suit.

I came back from Recsk in sombre mood. The concentration camp may have been a decade before the Inga and Janos story but the history of Hungary seems to be layered in hidden hurts and cruelties. Maybe the new openness will heal some of them. My third week here, time is moving too quickly. Tomorrow Lisa will get the translation. Too restless to sleep when I get back to my hotel room, I pour myself a glass of wine and switch on the TV. There is a western on one channel and a farming programme on the other. I turn the sound down low and flick from one to the other. When the farming programme finishes there is a documentary programme showing new blocks of lakotelep.

I feel depressed. What have I learned so far? That many women and men are called Janos and Gertrude. Even in that cramped space Granny had generated a sense of home and festivity as she tossed langos from the pan to the plate. All the people in that living room looked as if they belonged there, at ease with themselves and each other in spite of the physical constraints of the place. What did that atmosphere remind me of? I'd been puzzling over this on and off since then. And now just as the credits were fading on the lakotelep programme, it came to me. The Harty kitchen. Mrs Harty in her cottage kitchen during mealtimes, the place bursting at the seams with younger children, all talking and eating together. Crowded and noisy, but the informality and the constant talk gave an air of vitality. Janus, god of doorways, two-headed and confusing! The doorway into the cramped flat in the lakotelep was one of close domesticity. How could so many people live in such little space? In spite of the air of hospitality generated by the grandmother, there must be many tensions behind such overcrowding. Day to day tensions that build and build. And the doorway in Recsk? Nothing now but a few concrete blocks, the pine forests and blue skies softening its impact. I think of 'Field End'. Its familiarity reassures me. Rockabye is probably looking out the nursery window at this very minute disdaining the mess I left in the room. I feel a sudden, overwhelming guilt about that. Aunt Em used to say,

'It's easy to know if a child has been reared properly. All you have to do is look at its bedroom.'

She meant inspect when she said 'look'.

'All children like a bit of mess. It gives them a sense of belonging. Nothing very much happens in a too-tidy room.' Aunt Alice would defend the state of my room, time and time again.

What am I doing here? Maybe Sam is right and I've flipped but I don't know it. I had a terrible crying jag on the way back from Recsk. It came from nowhere. Ann thought I was upset by the horror stories Lisa was telling us. Case histories of inmates of Recsk. But it wasn't that at all. The music called up my dead baby. If it had been born it would be ten months and three days old now. If?

I'm tired. I turn off the TV. I get a cup of drinking chocolate from the drinks machine but it's thin and watery. I leave it half-finished and get ready for bed. I don't attempt counting sheep tonight. Instead, I close my eyes and fall asleep, for some reason dreaming of Aunt Alice's thin white tea service.

I wake to loud knocking. It's Lisa.

'Aren't you even dressed?' she looks me up and down contemptuously. 'My first story of the day is with the editor and you've still got sleep in your eyes.'

'Sorry,' I mumble. 'I remember my wake up call but I must have drifted off again.'

'I'm picking up the translation now. You wanna come?'

'Yes. I won't be a minute,' and I dash off to the bathroom to splash my face with water and put on some clothes.

The translator lives on Vatci Utca, in the building opposite the Adidas shop, as it turns out. I notice the queue even though it's only ten in the morning. We take the lift to the fifth floor and ring the bell of the third apartment. The door is opened by a black haired woman. Her name is Katya. She has the delicate features and long curly hair of a Pre-Raphaelite. Her eyes are a deep blue. Lisa makes the introductions and we're invited in. The drawing room of the apartment is startlingly austere. Bauhaus furniture, its clear clean lines are the only intrusion in this white walled room. The floor is covered in black tiles, so highly polished that at a quick glance it might be mistaken for glass. There are no pictures on the walls. She picks a single sheet of paper from a table and passes it to Lisa. I glance at it.

'I am sorry that there is so little. There are many repetitions in this piece. Many times the same thing is repeated in awkward Hungarian by someone who does not speak the language perhaps.'

Her English is stilted but in a charming way. She looks from me to Lisa.

'I have listed in brackets how many times these phrases are repeated.'

Such thoroughness numbs any immediate response I might have had. I look at the page in Lisa's hands, as if by looking, it will multiply on the page.

'I have prepared coffee in my kitchen,' she points in the direction of a presumably immaculate kitchen.

'No thanks,' Lisa replies for both of us, 'I've gotta get back to the office.' She hands Katya an envelope and we leave.

We don't speak going down in the lift. It clanks and wheezes noisily. Lisa still has the page. 'We'll go to Gerbeaud's to read it,' she says in an authoritative tone.

'What about the office?'

'Katya's a terrific translator but lousy company over coffee.'

We order coffee and cakes and bend our heads in tandem to the page. It reads:

Hungary is a flat country (five times)
A cork is hilly (five times)
Inga (three times)
Sarah (ten times)

Janos (once)
John (ten times)
Gertrude (five times)
Deirdre (ten times)
Refugee (twenty times)
Sometimes I feel like a refugee.
Collect clothes and take to camp.
Mud, cold, hunger.
These people have such spirit.
Belonging (ten times)
Home (five times)
Where?
My father was stern (ten times)
Am I a stern father? I hope not.
Sarah is a mother.
Inga is a mother.
I am happy.

'There's so little,' I protest.

'Maybe not,' Lisa cajoles. 'This probably means more than it suggests at a first reading. Now, I really have to get to the office. Will you be alright? Why not give Ann a buzz? She'll mooch about with you if she's not practising new steps. Might as well see as much of the city as you can. Only two days left.'

I pretend a cheerfulness I don't feel.

'I'm fine. I'll ring Ann after I finish my coffee,' I wave her off and turn my attention once more to the sheet of paper in my hand.

I don't ring Ann. Her burbling jocularity would get on my nerves right now. She still hasn't left for Oregon. Lisa suspects that there's more to Ann than this innocent folkdancer we see before us.

'She's CIA. I used to date one of their guys,' she whispered in conspiratorial tones last night after dinner.

'Are you crazy? You said yourself she hasn't a word of the language and she keeps getting lost on trams and subways.'

'A clever front. It's all part of the training.'

'That's the maddest thing I've heard in a long time.'

'It's not as mad as you wanting to be Hungarian.'

When I look at Katya's page, evidence of Hungarian origins is thin. I remember when I was ten years old Mam knit me a jumper in a murky brown. It was from a book of patterns called *Tough Tops for Climbers*. I loved it. Mostly because of the title of the pattern book. I ran about the yard and fields repeating 'tough tops for climbers,' over and over. An incantation of delight.

'The most you've ever climbed is Giant's Stone and everyone knows a dwarf kicked that into place. You look a right eejit,' Greta said.

Two months later, Harty bought Mrs Harty a knitting machine for their eleventh wedding anniversary. He'd come up and down to the house for weeks with the catalogue. He'd read aloud from it in the kitchen while Mrs Harty baked.

'New Wonder Auto Knitter, yours for only £2 18s 6d deposit and eight monthly payments of £3 6s 6d or £26 13s 6d cash. Fully automatic with automatic wool feed, unbreakable all steel needle bed. No risk, full guarantee plus free tuition at home.'

Mrs Harty got her machine and she made Greta a 'tough top for climbers'. I wanted to say, 'You look a right eejit,' but of course I didn't.

3

THE TRUTH, SUCH AS IT IS

'HELLO, DODOS,' Greta in a minuscule red bikini is perched on the kitchen table, peeling an orange. Her legs dangle on air.

'How was London?'

'Sweltering. Busy.'

I plonk the duty free bags and the plastic bags from Harrods on the table next to her. A gin bottle rolls sideways but I catch it.

'I like goodees,' Greta says abandoning her orange juice and raiding the bags, 'Why don't you tell me what you've been up to while I fix you a stiff drink? Your hair is a holy show by the way.'

Up to, is right. I'm tempted to tell her about the waiter but I don't. He had an afternoon off and I didn't want to ring Ann. Katya's page depressed me. He wanted to come to my hotel room but I said his place or not at all. The room was the size of a cupboard and was stiflingly warm.

When I saw it, I wanted to change my mind but in the end I said nothing. He was fast and I was furious. One of those encounters where 'sordid' is an apt description. There was a time I would have told her about it. A few months ago but not now. How things change!

Belonging

Greta is on her feet and reaching into a cupboard for glasses. She always behaves as if you've left the room a moment ago and returned for something or other. It used to drive me crazy but I've grown used to it over the years.

'I don't see any for sale sign.'

'What?'

'For sale, as in *House for sale*.'

'Oh that? I haven't had time and I'm not sure I want to sell.'

'Time?' Her eyebrows arch a question but I won't rise to that bait. 'It seems to me you've had nothing but time. From May to the end of July is a huge chunk of time, whatever way you look at it.'

'You may be looking at it in a completely different way to me. Do you remember when the boys' junior school was closed because of the strike?'

'What has that got to do with this? Of course I remember it. But that was years ago. Our Billy was at home for a full month and we had to go to school and be tortured by namby-pamby nuns as usual. If truth be known our building was even damper than theirs, except the good sisters hadn't the guts to go on strike. They should have pulled our school down the same time they bulldozed the boys' one.'

'I remember Father Fahy read out a letter from the Department of Education at mass about it saying that 'everything possible would be done to expedite its reconstruction as the urgency of the need for a new school was fully appreciated.'

'Have you finally gone round the bend?'

'I don't think so. You're the one who has been urging me to sell. I'm not sure that's what I want to do. There's no rising damp here. I don't have to sell this house. The nuns' school is still standing and the 'new' boys' school is falling to pieces.'

'Is this a moral tale of conservation?'

'Maybe, maybe not. But things are never as straight forward as they seem.'

'You're telling me!'

'How have you been?'

I'm anxious to change the topic. Greta has a happy knack of getting her own way in most conversations.

'Anytime I rang before going to London I talked to some strange man with very little English.'

Greta splashes a drink in my direction, skidding it across the table like they do in Western movies.

'Just like Ma. Judgmental about any man in my life. Well, fairy princess, while you've been dreaming away in the Celtic twilight here, I've been slaving in Mammon's great maw, racing to and from rehearsals as usual and . . .' She slurps her orange juice noisily and the pause grows, 'and I've been babysitting Barry.'

'Why? Has he regressed to childhood since I left?'

'Seems to me, kiddo, that you're the one who has regressed. What's with camping in the nursery?'

'I like it there.'

'If Mark could see it . . .' her voice trails into laughter. 'All those sessions and it's back to old Rockabye. Maybe life is circular after all. He's been talking to your answering machine since you left.'

'Really!'

'Every Tuesday and Thursday Mark rings. He's regular, I'll say that for him.'

'A regular jerk.'

'No analyst likes to lose a patient. Barry thinks he

needs help.'

'Why? Can't he pick up food from Frank's deli without me?'

'Not Barry. Mark. He's worried about him.'

'Then let him worry if that's what he wants to do. I'm sorry I couldn't take Concorde to be with him twice a week. If Barry wants something to worry about he should start thinking about the massacre in Tiananmen Square. Something worthwhile, not a tinpot analyst. He's missing sleeping with me, that's all. Barry should tell him to get lost.'

'He doesn't know about your unprofessional relationship and he doesn't want to upset your healer.'

'Physician heal thyself is what I say at this point.'

'He sang to the answering machine the last time he rang. That really freaked Barry.'

'Why, was it an Irish song?'

'No. *I Will Survive*. I think it was the choice of song rather than the singing that upset him.'

Greta hums the tune, then does her Tina Turner interpretation of the chorus, growling out the words. I join in. My eyes skim by her head. The fat Madonna and Child now hangs by the dresser. The placid Baby Jesus is smiling at me. He too wants to sing.

'That picture,' I point to it when we come to a stop, 'how long has it been there? It used to be in the drawing room.'

'I moved it in here for Ma. It's always been a favourite of hers. I didn't think you'd mind. She likes to look at it when she works.'

'Then she must have it,' I say emphatically.

I take it from the wall.

'I've never liked it. It reminds me of tortuous speech

classes on Tuesdays and Thursdays with Miss Bateman. Remember her?'

'Yea. Navy suits and a wig.'

'It wasn't a wig. You're wicked. Close curls, a tight perm.'

'Disciplined hair then, no need to rush to her defence. You hated her.'

'The classes were an endurance test and that picture was a witness to all my humiliations. It hung above the piano. Remember her play and sing routine? She played, I sang.'

'Ma won't want to take it. You know what she's like. She only wanted to look at it. Old Batesy did her bit though. You were Shirley Temple by the time she finished with you.'

'Some Shirley Temple! Fluid speech was as remote from me as dimples.'

'What are you doing?'

'I'm giving the fat child and Madonna their marching papers. Mrs Harty will have to take it. It's a gift. I'll insist,' I say as I wrap it inexpertly in brown paper and twine. Panic rises. I'd like to get it out of the house this minute.

'I've outgrown it,' I say as nonchalantly as possible, 'just as I've outgrown Miss Bateman.'

'Ah! but have you outgrown your Tuesdays and Thursdays with Mark?'

The question is a slap in the face. I'd never made the connection before. Tuesdays and Thursdays with Miss Bateman, Tuesdays and Thursdays with Mark. Bullseye Greta. 'You tell me. He's been talking to my answering machine for months. I wrote one note to him since I left. What do you think?'

I'm not sure if my voice is steady. Sudden tiredness makes me aware of all my bones. I examine the rows of cups in the dresser. 'Pender blue lake' crowds its shelves. Dad's last line, the one he designed before Tom took over the reins in 1967. I don't want to lock eyes or horns with Greta. Budapest seems centuries away. Janos, Janos and Janos, a trinity of grotesques from a fevered imagining.

'I think you've been up to something, Miss.'

I laugh in spite of myself. It's what Mrs Harty used to say to us when she was cross. She said it the day we locked Aunt Em's handbag into the cupboard in the pantry. Aunt Em was giving one of her dressmaking demonstrations in Kinsale, at the Municipal Hall. Greta and myself made the posters for her.

Dressmaking Demonstration
in
Kinsale Municipal Hall
Thursday next 7 February
at 2.00 pm
The cutting of dresses, suits and coats
will be demonstrated.
Pattern books on sale.
Silver collection taken.
Proceeds in aid of Nash Lodge,
home to distressed Protestant Gentlewomen.

We wanted to go with her. Not to the demonstration but for a day out in Kinsale. She wouldn't hear of it. We hid her handbag. Car keys and money and her best patterns were in it. There was consternation but we kept our mouths shut. In the end, Mam rang Dad at the factory. He came home and drove Aunt Em to Kinsale.

Mam found the handbag in the pantry cupboard before the day was out.

Mrs Harty proclaimed her innocence. Aunt Alice put the bag at the end of Aunt Em's wardrobe and when she came home she was extremely embarrassed when she discovered it. If only what I was up to now was as simple as hiding a handbag.

'You're right,' I say lightly. 'I've been spending more money than I should. Tara, Geraldine and I took London by storm.'

'And how are the old creeps? I can never remember one from the other. The breeder and the babyless one. They're all a jumble to me, never having met them.'

'God, you're heartless.' I fly to Tara and Geraldine's defence.

'Here, let me give you a refill.'

'It's only two in the afternoon, I don't think . . .'

'Not in Tokyo, it isn't. Anyway, we haven't seen each other for months. I really missed you.'

'Then join me in a drink. If you're pouring the stuff down my throat, the least you can do is keep me company.'

'I have to watch the calories. We're not all as lucky as you. Eat and drink what you like and still look like a beanpole.'

'Thanks a bundle. I can tell you really missed me. That's why you kept returning my phonecalls.'

'You know I can't deal with long distance stuff. I thought about you every day and talked to Barry about you a few times a week.'

'Really! Have you been seeing a lot of each other then?'

'Not exactly going out to dinner but he's been

babysitting for me. Zelda left the neighbourhood, left the country, in fact. She's in Canada with her daughter. The one with the twins. I always thought she'd retire to Vienna. She talked about it often enough. "My heart belongs in Vienna, I merely exist in New York." And now she's gone north and left me high and dry. And you know how long it takes to get a reliable replacement sitter. That guy will make a terrific dad.'

The subtlety of an axe, that's Greta. I see my unborn baby's fingers peep from a cauldron and I'm the bad witch stirring the brew.

'I thought you said you had been babysitting him but it appears he's fallen in love with Cáit and Róisín. Younger women were always his style. Where are they, by the way?'

'With their Dad, Brian Boru, the great Voiceover. We really miss Zelda. You hear such horror stories about babysitters in New York.'

'A lot of them are apocryphal. Remember the one about the drug addict putting the baby in the microwave?'

'Keep talking, friend. You're making me feel terrific. I advertised and interviewed for a replacement but so far, zilch. The references didn't pan out on two of them and the other one had too rigid an approach. She'd have been perfect if the kids were robots.'

'At least you won't have to worry about babysitters when you're here.'

'True, the Voiceover has a heavy schedule planned for them and Bella has invited them for a weekend to Midleton. They'll probably spend the time in the stables. They're both pony mad at present. Just like we were at that stage.'

'Yes.' I don't want to talk horses with Greta.

'Cáit wants a pony of her own. Can you imagine? A horse in the attic in the Village! Very New York. She says we don't have to keep it in the apartment. Seven year olds have perfect logic. I felt like telling her we can hardly afford the apartment but I bit my tongue back. Harty was always preaching economy when I was a kid. I don't want to dump the same rubbish on Cáit and Róisín.'

'But the Voiceover has always been prompt with maintenance, hasn't he?'

'Yea, I've been lucky there. I can't grouch really. The thing is, I didn't know how expensive agency sitters were until Zelda went. I've obviously been underpaying her for years. We cried buckets at her going-away party. That stuff-shirt brother turned up.'

'The attorney?'

'Yea. The one who put all his money into property.'

'Did he bring his new wife?'

'The child-bride didn't come. She was probably at home brushing up on her finger painting. You could tell Zelda didn't want him there. He stuck out like a sore thumb. He didn't belong. The living room was packed with seven to ten year olds and resting actors and Mr Attorney was walking about in an immaculate white suit. He shrieked any time a pair of sticky hands came his way.'

'And did he tough it out to the end?'

'Almost. Zelda took him aside and thanked him for coming after we cut the cake and took photos. She said she was staying overnight, so he headed home to the baby-bride and cartoon time.'

I've finished my drink and I'm beginning to feel a bit

woozy. There's no sign of Mrs Harty about the place.

'And where's Mrs Harty?'

'Harty put his back out. She's whisked him off to a faith healer somewhere between here and Kerry. They took Lally and Tim with them. Ma packed a hamper. They'll picnic on the way. She left a casserole for you. Said you'd like some proper food after London.'

'I'm not hungry. It must be the heat but after a few more sips of this I might need some sustenance. Have you seen Sam?'

'I've seen Dr Livingstone. He's been parading about in khaki shorts to the consternation of the parish. They like their tycoons in suits around here. He's camping with Marge.'

'I thought he'd have left by now.'

'They went yesterday. Tom, Marge, Sam and the two prodigies. Those two kids are too smart for their own good. I've put my finger on what irritates me about them.'

'And what's that?'

'They have insolent good manners, the kind calculated to make an adult feel uneasy.'

'You were never keen on civilities.'

'Thanks a bundle. I'll crawl back into my cave and practise my grunts. Anyway, they loaded up the jeep and headed for rougher frontiers. Tom said they couldn't waste a full weekend indoors in weather like this. They send their regards.'

'I had a row with Sam. Well not exactly a row. More like a disagreement really.'

'Oh yeah! I heard you took all your clothes off.'

'Has Sam been talking to you? I wanted to show him my bones.'

'Great show by all accounts.'

The gin is beginning to hit me and I feel teary.

'It wasn't like that at all.'

'Forget it, Dodos. I'm not puritanical.'

'Shut . . .' Nothing comes. Trapped, I shake my head vigorously. I stand up and move about. I look at the brown package. Madonna and pudgy Jesus. It's leaning against the dresser. I pull the wrapping off and sing to the baby,

'I didn't want to do it, I didn't want to do it.'

Greta sings along, 'He can hear you and so can I. The boy-child might buy it but sorry not I.'

I must be really drunk I think as I outstare the baby Jesus eyeball to eyeball.

'I don't care what you believe,' I hear my voice childishly insistent. 'I wanted him to see me as I am. neither he nor Marge believes Dad's journal. But I do and that's all that matters.'

'So, you took all your clothes off and chopped your hair to bits to make a point.'

'You must've had a long talk with Marge and Sam then.' My resentment can't be hidden.

'They're worried about you. So am I and Ma puts your trip to London down to her prayers. She said you were stuck indoors for weeks before that.'

I put the picture back against the dresser and park myself on Mrs Harty's rocking chair, the one she's sat in for decades when the day's work is done.

'Put some casserole into a bowl for me. I'd better eat something. I haven't eaten yet today.'

'Okay, Miss Muck.'

We could be ten years old again, Greta ready to bully and scold. Old patterns die hard. I shouldn't have had that second gin on an empty stomach. It's tiredness too of course. The morning I left Budapest, Lisa and Ann insisted on a little spree. They twirled me in and out of shops on the Parisi Udvar. I didn't want to shop and we had been out late the night before at a Haydn concert at the Fertod Castle, a magical confection of baroque architecture. The setting and the music went to my head even before champagne at the interval. We made a last call to Gerbeaud's for a pastry before I left.

When I boarded the plane for London, I felt so full I couldn't imagine ever eating again. Even though I had an overnight stay I didn't eat. The following morning I raced around shops in Oxford Street buying things I didn't need. Hard to explain a shopping trip to London if you come back empty handed.

The casserole is wonderful and I eat like a greedy child. Lamb, carrots, potatoes with a hint of oregano and some peppers. Delicious.

'Now that you've filled your belly, you should be able to give me some account of what's really going on here.'

'Nothing's going on. I've been away for a few weeks in London, that's all.'

'I'm not talking about that and you know it.' Impatience makes her look mean and cold. 'You're still not going on with this craziness about the journal. That you're Hungarian? Your father was always a bit odd. Never dealt with the real world, did he?'

'My father was Hungarian. His name was Janos.'

The fantasy is voiced and even I'm shocked. But Greta's aggressive truculence has forced my hand. I won't go back on it now. Retreats are painful. Her laugh is flinty. 'I've heard it all now. Sam is right. He thinks you're having a nervous breakdown. Your father was a kindly doddery old man. He hid himself away from life in this house. He hid behind things.' Her voice has risen, her eyes rake the kitchen as if to look for some confirmation for what she's saying. 'He hid behind his collections; stamps, pipes, snuff boxes, vases. He loved beautiful things. He loved his delicate wife and he loved you. That's the start and finish of it. How you think that such a timid man as he could organise something so utterly fantastic is beyond me.'

'But not beyond me,' I reply casually. It's an effort but I don't want anymore of this.

Greta ignores this totally.

'You've always worked yourself into the ground. It was bound to catch up with you. And then the shock of two deaths. You're going through a form of hysterical denial, that's all. You don't want to believe your parents are dead so you've invented new ones. But you can't go on like this much longer. Decisions will have to be taken and you'll have to face up to them.'

'I know and I have.' I agree, but I do not press my conclusions again.

'Good,' she flashes her headmistressy smile. The one that forgives the recalcitrant student even though she has burned down the school. 'I knew you'd see sense once I got here. Why don't we go out to the terrace?'

And she heads off through the house without even a backward glance. Greta strides forward, glad she's brought the outcast to heel. I know I should be angry but I don't want to waste energy. I'm beginning to face the fact that some decisions will have to be taken but they're not the ones that Greta has so neatly mapped out for me. I don't know if I want to hang out a *For sale* sign. I feel travel-stained and sticky but if I had a bath and a nap Greta would interpret that as withdrawal. At least I've eaten. I cheer myself with that thought as I follow her to the terrace.

He's there. Sitting bolt upright on a green cane chair. In cream T-shirt and shorts, a can of Guinness in his hand. First Sam, now Barry. Appearing suddenly without warning.

'Surprise!' he says, his face a toothy smile, the blue eyes giving me the once over 'I'm a day early. I thought you'd be pleased.'

Barry. It couldn't be August yet, could it?

'July 31st instead of August 1st,' he says as if he can mind-read. He doesn't stand up or come towards me and I find I'm resisting going towards him too.

'That's fine,' I lie. 'Been gadding about too much, lost track of time.'

'What did you do to your lovely hair?' He's peeved. One would have thought I'd cut his. Delilah to his Samson.

'I cut it because I felt like it,' I notice the hedge clippers by his chair. 'You've been cutting the hedges, I see. They look very neat. Standing to attention in fact. They never looked like that before. I've always preferred the wild look myself.'

'It's the *Dangerous Liaisons* look,' Greta says from the depths of the hammock, 'the film, all formal gardens and torrid passions.'

I'm strangely inhibited by them. Their combined presence makes me want to withdraw. Greta swings lightly to and fro. Not being able to see her, just the bulge of her body shaping the hammock makes what she contributes to the conversation carry more weight.

A hidden Cassandra. I am shocked to see how tall and handsome Barry is. A Viking American. Blond, blue-eyed and six foot two. Not a spare inch of flesh to be seen. Exercised muscles and a golden tan. The shorts emphasise the length of leg. He's barefoot, his long toes taking the heat from the red terrace tiles. My feet feel puffy as if they overflow my shoes. I'm surprised when I look down and they don't. My stomach is heavy with Mrs Harty's casserole. It drags on me like the wolf with the bellyful of stones.

'How're things, Dee?' He's smiling, a lazy smile that invites intimacy.

'Okay.'

'She bought Harrods,' Greta's disembodied voice talks as if I'm not there, 'Dodos has always bought too much in shops. I remember when she got her first pay cheque in New York, she blew it all on silk pyjamas and a wool coat. Drank tinned soup for a month. I threw her the odd lamb chop but she was quite happy prancing about the apartment in her pyjamas, no money to go anywhere.'

'Don't call me Dodos.'

'I've always called you Dodos. It's an affectionate term.'

'It's an extinct animal.'

'Well, you might as well have been extinct for the last few months as far as Barry and I were concerned.'

'I rang and wrote to Barry every week,' I'm defensive but I can't help it.

'Yea, short notes, a few lines.'

'Have you been reading his letters then?' I look at Barry when I say this. His eyes slide downwards and he concentrates on his drink.

'We saw a bit of each other because of the children.'

'I never knew Barry and you had children.'

I wish Barry would look at me. Is there gold in the can of Guinness? His knuckles around the can are tensed to whiteness, as if all his energies are concentrated on it. I could have stayed in London for a few more days, recovered from Budapest before returning. Now, I'm sorry I didn't. 'I've been teaching Cáit and Róisín the tin whistle.' His voice is matter of fact.

'I suppose the alien joined in.'

'The alien?' Barry's confused.

'Greta's man, the one with no English.'

'Stefan has been gone for weeks . . .' it's the hammock voice . . . 'I was only helping him out until he found a place of his own. He's an actor.'

'But he fills his time between parts waiting table,' I finish for her.

'How did you know?' It's a genuine enquiry.

'We know each other a long time,' I say and stand up.

Barry stands too, as if remembering old world etiquette. I want to lie down and sleep. I'm spun out, need to be on my own. I know too little and too much about everything but one thing I'm sure of, I'm not going to participate in other people's games when they won't even recognise change or confusion in me. Except to see these changes as a malady, something to be gotten out of the system, to be put behind me before I come to my senses. I'm looking down at Greta. Her face has that still quietness of a child sure of itself and awaiting experiences in the certainty that they will be enjoyable. For the first time, it seems strange to me that

Greta's face is unmarked by the pains that I know she has suffered. At thirty-two, she could pass for a decade younger, and frequently does, particularly in the parts she plays on stage. Young women, beautiful but flawed, victims of their own personalities or the men they share their lives with. 'I'm off to bed,' I say and I move towards the French windows.

'Will I come?' Barry asks, a giant child asking permission.

'Only if you want to tuck me in,' I neatly invert the roles. 'I want to sleep.'

'Sure, kiddo,' he adapts quickly.

We troop silently through the house, then climb the two stairs to the nursery. I know I should have left him with the ingenue in the hammock. It's large enough for both of them to swing in. But we're at the nursery door. I've grown older on the journey through the house. Old. Ancient. The oldest woman in the world. A survivor who has been through the wars and wears her wrinkles as trophies, a necklace of lines on the neck. I stop outside the door and turn to Barry and wonder why he doesn't wince at my decay. He is like a cub scout, all innocent cleanliness and order, a boy-child in short pants on his first trip to the woods. The room is orderly. Mrs Harty's ministrations, I presume. Stuffed toys stand to attention on the window seats. Rockabye has been turned towards the window to give him a view. The objects on Dad's desk no longer crowd it but are neatly on parade. The narrow bed beckons a child, the patchwork quilt a homely invitation.

'This is really cute, Dee,' Barry is walking about picking things up and putting them down again. Now that he's indoors, I see that he's regained adulthood. In fact, his huge maleness threatens, dwarfs everything, even Dad's desk. He sits on the chair at the desk and it suddenly becomes a miniature doll's table, the wicked giant with his mighty hand could splinter it in seconds.

'Don't,' I squawk throatily as he investigates the inkpot stand.

He looks at me alarmed.

'Sorry, please don't move anything about. I have them in a special order,' I lie.

'That's really weird, kiddo, since I helped Mrs Harty fix this place up last night and it was in one hell of a mess.'

'Okay, I confess . . . just stop fidgeting. I'm tired.'

I step out of my dress and underwear and go to the tiny sink to wash. He's sitting on the bed watching me but I pretend I don't know. The cold flannel feels good and already I feel less tired. I glance at Barry in the mirror above the little basin and realise how much I've missed him. I towel myself slowly. I'm waiting for him to say something but he doesn't. I walk towards the bed. He's sitting on the edge. I sit astride him playfully in earnest, all thoughts of being chastely tucked in for sleep in the remote long ago. I had forgotten his smell. How could that happen? He smells deliciously of cinnamon. We've often talked about our smells, his cinnamon, mine heather. Idled over their distinctiveness. I cannot smell my heather. He cannot smell his cinnamon.

I've always loved cinnamon. I include it in every culinary concoction I can, from apple tarts to meat dishes. Now, I want to eat him up without preamble. I lick his teeth. We tumble like children on a hilltop on the tilted nursery floor. His kisses are so moist and vast

I feel I could disappear down his throat. The wall stops us and we laugh, falling apart suddenly. Then we roll towards each other again.

'I want to see all of you. It's so long since I've looked at you like this,' he says.

I feel suddenly self-conscious and want to hide from his eyes. I think of my tummy, plump from Gerbeaud's pastries and the dark birth mark on my right thigh. I want to be covered up. I reach past him to the bed and shake the patchwork quilt to the floor to cover us.

'Babes in the woods,' he says as we nestle and nuzzle under cover. I look towards the barred windows and I can see the treetops moving gently.

'Look at the trees,' I point in their direction. 'We're in a treehouse.'

It's dusk when I wake. My bones ache and my right arm has gone dead. Barry's golden head is lying in the crook of my arm. A dead weight. I shake him with my free hand. His eyes blink rapidly.

'Greta,' he calls.

'Just move your head, Barry. My arm's numb.'

I push him from me and move my arm about vigorously. Pins and needles in my arms, deadness in my heart. I knew before he muttered her name. Knew the minute I stepped on to the terrace, when she lolled out of sight in the hammock and he sat upright in the cane chair. Knew when he didn't come towards me then.

'Dee?'

'I'm not Dee or Dodos, I'm Gertrude,' I say gently but firmly.

'Gertrude?'

'Oh, for heaven's sake, does everything have to be a

question with you? You know yourself and Greta have talked about all this. Why pretend?'

He doesn't answer at first.

'Greta doesn't talk, she tells you things. You listen and they seem fine at the time.' His voice is flat.

I have told Barry that it doesn't matter. But in such a way that he knows it does. Not the sleeping with Greta. No. Sleeping with men is not serious stuff with Greta. I understand her. We understand each other to a lesser or greater degree. It's Barry's babysitting that I can't forgive. The thoughts of cosy bedtime stories and the *en famille* tenderness; that's what cuts through me. Now is the summer of my discontent and the bastards are playing happy families. I see Greta, Barry and me, a triptych framed by a yellow cab en route from the abortion clinic and I know they have spotlighted my fear just as surely as my luminous Madonna from Knock must have lit up Dad's misery. Mark says my litany of woes keeps me going but then therapists always take the obvious view. My disappointment with him no longer rankles. In fact, he's fading into the brain's remote skyways — a chartered flight taken for economy but by its nature a let-down. All my budgeting for Tuesdays and Thursdays with Mark has paid off less than my torment by Miss Bateman in the dining room of childhood.

Even by the time I made my confirmation — a day stitched into memory — I still couldn't talk easily. Mam made me a full length dress of raw silk with delicate embroidery of the Pender emblem, fronds of ferns in a wild spray. *Maximus in minimis* — very great in very small things — the family motto, bordered the hem. She laboured for months on the dress. When the day came I was very relieved to get out of the dress after church and the reception. It pulled on my body like polio irons. Greta, resplendent in a cotton dress with a Pender lace collar, outshone me. She chatted to my ancient relatives in a comradely fashion that had them fighting for her attention. All I wished for was hot chocolate and bed, some time to chew my thumb in comfort, away from all Penders and of course, Greta.

Now I imagine her haloed by night time, Cáit and Róisín asleep (thumbsuckers, both), Barry awaiting her return to the apartment in the Village. The interior of Greta's apartment changes with a speed and style that would be exhausting to anyone less energetic. It's been country cottage, all stripped pine and open shelves; African primitive, blank white walls and free-standing enormous tribal sculptures; Japanese high tech, spare black narrow furniture, grey carpets, two chairs and an origami arrangement per room. Last time I was in it, it was kitsch baroque. Papier mâché moulded ceilings, columns bedecked with silk flowers, cascades of curtains and over-ornate lamps that threw a honeyed romantic glow. It's this interior I imagine her returning to with that breathless vitality that is her trademark.

Barry gives her a drink. She entertains him over a late night supper by dissecting the leading actor's unhappy love life. They both look in fondly at the children asleep before they tumble on to Greta's four poster bed surrounded by the sickly mural of a lady and gentleman beautifully got up in frills and flounces sitting under an umbrella in eternal sunshine. She used to have a water bed and the walls were painted like a Jacques Cousteau still, shot from the ocean's floor. Before that it was an enormous hammock swinging in a pseudo desert island setting, palm trees and painted monkeys.

I am mooning with Lally, Mrs Harty's youngest daughter, on the swing near the orchard. She's reading. I keep us going. Just a gentle push every minute or so. She accepts my presence easily. I don't talk, that's the key to it. I can imagine I'm back with Greta on this swing. Like years ago but more peaceful. There's no pinching this time around. Greta complains.

'That Lally's a strange one, Ma. Her head's in a book from morning to night.'

'She's book-clever, that's all. Harty and myself tried to stop her but she was reading in outhouses and not gettin' fresh air, so, we let her be.'

Barry has hired a car, a Rover. Every day it's a new trip. He's even bundled Mrs Harty into it a few times and taken her and Greta to the sea. I have kept myself separate from these excursions. I wave them off and welcome them home. They fit well together and are full of stories of the day's wanderings when they return. I plead work as my excuse. I say I have to post off a couple of lectures a week to my Head of Department. Truth is, all my texts are in New York and I send off literary magazines in jiffy bags to salve my conscience. Irina is quite happy with my absence. My substitute is paid at the lowest rate possible and the department is saving money. She's even suggested a sabbatical. I've never taken one but now as the summer wears on and I'm as muddled as ever, it seems impossible that I will return to New York at the end of the month. I tell Irina I will ring by August 15th with my decision. Barry thinks I will return with him at the end of his holiday or at least he pretends he does. In the meantime he has away days with Greta and sometimes with Mrs Harty and young Tim too. Happy families. I moon. Lally reads and swings. I'm in Cork but I'm imagining Budapest. Lisa has written twice since my return. Her letters attracted Mrs Harty's curiosity. When she asks about her, I say, 'A New York journalist who's covering all the new changes in Eastern Europe these days.'

'What's her name?' Greta pipes up.

We're in the kitchen unloading the picnic basket after their day trip to Kinsale.

'Lisa Pennington. I met her at NYU when she was covering the Virginia Woolf conference in '85,' I lie.

Barry is shaking the gingham tablecloth out the back door to rid it of crumbs and other accretions.

'Give it a thorough shaking, Barry,' Mrs Harty encourages him from the sink.

'I met her,' he says casually without turning his head in my direction. The gingham is in full sail. An Irish summer wind could carry him skywards.

'She knows Stirkov. She's a girlfriend of his. She did the write-up on the international folk festival in Oregon.'

The world contracts and my stomach with it. I remember the music in Recsk. That same music in the apartment in Spring Street. The day I came back from the clinic.

'Stirkov says she could have been first class but she couldn't hack the solo circuit. She left music for journalism. Said it was less competitive. Isn't that nutty? He's really into her. He was on a downer there for a while when she pulled out of New York. He's dating this real bimbo to fill in his time between her trips home.'

'I'd like to meet her,' Greta says. She knows there's something askew here and she zones in. She's at a loss and I'm glad. Barry reassures her.

'Next time she's in New York, we'll call you, won't we, Dee?'

'Mmm,' I assent casually. I know now that I will take Irina's sabbatical. It's not enough that I've decamped to the nursery. Not enough that I sleep with Paddington Bear, not to mention the away days. This woman has found a secret cubbyhole and she wants me to hand over the key.

I placate instead of demonstrate. I offer home-made lemonade. A salve. A Lally-Dee triumph that will quench begrudgery as well as thirst. Lally, silent listener, partner in alienation has read her way through the facts about Stone-Age civilization while we've talked. She tilts her head upwards in recognition when I praise her lemonade-making skills. She smiles. A narrow smile, watching itself. I recognise a sister.

Lisa can get me an apartment in Vatci Utca, the Grafton Street of Budapest. A genuine place to live. A flat to set out from and come home to. But I am cowardly. Curiously unable to express my own wishes, at least not yet openly. I store them up, wear camouflage, wait.

'We had a wow of a day in Kinsale today. Greta's a terrific sailor.'

He's showing off. The biggest kid on the block marking out his territory.

'I just followed instructions,' Greta, the acolyte, who knows she's not, replies.

'Tim threw up,' Mrs Harty offers her tuppence worth.

I laugh, suddenly lightweight and freed from everything humdrum, even gravity. I will play mouse. I will stay in my chewed-out hole and await opportunity. I do not have to respond to the first piece of gnawed cheese thrown my way. I will be circumspect. For this reason I can afford to be gracious.

'I want to take you all to tea at Butlers,' I say brightly.

A routine has established itself. If it's been an away-day, Barry, Greta and I go for a drink at the hotel in the evenings. Greta is drinking very little. Just a glass of wine and she drinks sparkling water after that. She says Mrs Harty's baking is adding enough poundage. I can't see it myself, but she's always been very disciplined about her weight. 'I'm not goin' to end up like Ma, small and round.'

Sometimes Sam and Marge join us but not Tom. Sam has stayed with Marge since my strip scene. He enjoyed meeting his old friends again, particularly, Rupert. Rupert Reddin (nicknamed Bear) has been spending weekends at Marge's. He's a big, burly, black-haired man, almost totally bald but with a compensatory biblical beard. Rachel and Simon have hooked him into their many hobbies, from science to sea-faring. He seems to love this 'uncle' role and he's promised the kids not to lose touch after Sam goes away.

Sam leaves next week. Marge has become younger in his presence. Twinned again, her matronliness has become less obvious. She laughs often and with ease. Sam and I have become polite acquaintances who must be careful not to be rude. It suits me, this retreat. Barry and he get along quite well. This irritates me though I can't think why. No, I lie. I know precisely why. Sam's behaviour towards me has rubbed off on Barry. When I'm in their company together I feel I'm seen as difficult but that if handled gently I can be guided towards good behaviour. I feel de-sexed, de-personalised. Yet, while this enrages, it also absolves me from continuous interaction. I merely have to be in their company. The less said, the better. My presence is enough participation. I can indulge my daydreams. Even have the odd snooze. Greta plays *femme fatale* with both of them and Marge has dropped matron for tomboy. Their interest in each other takes all their energy.

Quite often I leave early after one drink. The first time I did this Barry protested vehemently. He insisted on walking at least as far as the end of the village with me. Then we turned from each other with relief. I have fallen into the habit of going for a walk in the evenings with Lally. I pick her up from the orchard, her usual spot, and we head off in a lazy stroll through the fields towards her cottage. We rarely speak, though silence isn't absolute. It suits us better, that's all. I have given her my china collection, dolls' sets of crockery from the nursery. Also Mam's sewing basket. A dark oak affair with innumerable drawers and little ivory knobs. Dad gave it to Mam as an engagement present. Marge says Lally has a wonderful pair of hands. She cuts and designs like a natural. She's won school prizes for outfits spun from bits of end-roll material from the factory.

'What will you be when you grow up, Lally?' I ask tonight as we approach the Harty cottage. Mrs Harty's torso is framed by the kitchen window as she bends to a task.

'An adult,' Lally says in that quiet firm way of hers

without even pausing.

She's gone. Spare with words but never short of an answer. When I was her age I got tongue-tied if someone passing on the road said, 'How are you?'

* * *

'I felt abandoned,' Barry says.

We're lying on the nursery floor, the patchwork quilt covering us. I'm chewing a sugar barley sweet.

'His phonecalls, the regularity of Tuesdays and Thursdays was obscene somehow. I figured there must be something to it.'

I wish he'd shut up. I really don't give a damn why he slept with Greta, why he's still courting her here, visiting her nightly after I'm tucked in. It's the talking about it that gets me down.

'I had to force her to tell me in the end. She told me yesterday.'

'Nobody forces Greta. She does as she pleases,' I say mildly. I feel remote from this discussion, 'Let me read you this section. Forget about Greta.' I'm reading *Alice in Wonderland* aloud but he keeps talking about Greta. He's impervious to Alice's quandaries.

'It's the deception. I thought we were happy. How could you do that to me if we were happy?'

'I didn't do anything to you. It had nothing to do with you. Forget about Mark, he's just another sick shrink.'

'He needs help alright,' his tone is soft.

'He should be struck off,' I say forcefully, 'he's got quite a good therapist, I believe.'

'So you think this is funny. Some kinda game or

what?'

'I don't think about it at all.'

'Fine. You've been locked away here in some kinda time warp. It's about time you did some real thinking.'

'Why?'

'Because it affects all of us.'

'All?'

'Me, you,' then he stops himself.

'And Greta,' I add as if completing a rhyme.

He doesn't meet my eyes but he mumbles, 'I suppose so.'

'You mustn't feel bound to me, Barry. Conscience, such as it is, can make cowards of us all.'

'I don't know what you're talking about.'

'I think you do.'

'It's difficult, complicated.'

'Difficult maybe,' I agree, 'but simple enough surely if you know what you want.' I realise I'm echoing Lisa.

'The thing is, Dee,' the phrase hangs in the air, an irresolute anthem to simple misery. Now I know it's coming, it seems to have always been inevitable. That moment when your eyes follow the line of the axe curving towards wood and it's too late to scream 'halt!'

'The thing is,' he repeats, 'Greta and I seem to have . . .,' his voice fades to nothingness but I know the axe is still in his hand.

I won't help him. He wants wood to split. I won't carry the log basket.

'. . . seem to have found something.'

It amuses me that in times of high emotion or evasion a comfortable cliché is used.

'Something?' I let it hang in air, the branch cut off before it hits ground.

'Well, love, I suppose.' He's apologetic as if this will reverse the hurt.

'Love!'

'Yes.'

Conviction is building. Even I can see that. In my mind's eye, I see Greta in the paddock exercising Sandysocks, the misery of chicken pox preventing me from claiming him first.

'The thing is,' he totters on, the full log basket slowing his progress, 'we both feel badly about it. It's been a goddamn strain, I can tell you.'

'No kidding!' Bitterness coats my tongue before I know it. Is this grief over the loss of love or simply pique because Greta won? I don't know.

I pop another sugar barley into my mouth. I laugh to myself. I'll keep busy, I'll survive. Time to shine up a few clichés myself. Time to throw another Gulliver out of Lilliput.

'You'll have to go,' I say, pulling the quilt off both of us. I'm amazed to see full-grown bodies underneath. I move towards Rockabye.

Boyishly awkward he jumps from one foot to the other, as he slips into his shorts and T-shirt.

'Close the door,' my voice is as imperial as I can muster. He does not look back but the door is firmly shut. I move towards Rockabye and am reassured by his smooth sameness. Wood softened and shiny. I mount him.

'Rock a bye baby on the tree top when the wind blows the cradle will rock. When the bough breaks the cradle will fall and down will come baby and cradle and all.'

Belonging

* * *

There was more to it, of course. There always is. I rocked and rocked and that was what I needed. Forwards and backwards, over and over. There was a time when I preferred Sandysocks to Rockabye but that was before the fire in the stables. It was nobody's fault then either. Just something that happened. The stables burned down in the night, just as Greta burned for Barry. Or Barry burned for her. Back then I woke to smoke and flames in a night sky. When I knew that Sandysocks was dead, I couldn't sleep without waking from smoke-filled dreams and his insistent neighing. I still have that dream. He's locked in. The smoke is thick. He's kicking his stall and I can't hear him until it's too late. I didn't want another pony. My passion for Sandysocks had been all-consuming. I couldn't dilute that even in memory by owning or taking to heart another horse. No one understood that but I wasn't bothered.

Barry, Greta, myself and an actor called Brad took a vacation a couple of years back at a ranch in Nevada. It was one of those dude ranches. It offered riding and horseshoe pitching for holiday folk. They use this ranch as a set for cheap westerns from time to time. When we were there, we had the place almost to ourselves. The owners, Rita and Chuck, retired movie extras, lived in the main cabin. There were twenty small tourist cabins, most of them empty, except for half a dozen. Apart from riding the trails and playing cowboys and cowgirls, the main recreation in the evening after we'd had a few beers in the saloon was horseshoe pitching. Outside the saloon was a notice which read:

> *Customers on horseback will not be served.*
> *Dismount now!*

Every evening when we went to the saloon, Brad would read the sign aloud in a cowboy drawl and laugh heartily. Greta said,

'Now you know what happens actors in a long run. They get a kick out of the same lines night after night.'

When it came to the horseshoe pitching, Barry and I were paired against Greta and Brad. Chuck kept score. We beat them every night. Not by much. A few points, but enough for Brad to get really mad on our last night there. We went to the saloon as usual but he was really knocking back the beers.

'You've been cheatin' all week, you two, and I aim to even the score. Okay, Barry, you wanna smash up the saloon or you wanna take a walk outside?'

He was using his cowboy drawl and at first I thought he was joking. He wasn't. He punched Barry in the face and laughed manically. Barry keeled over, just like in the movies. Chuck had to frogmarch Brad to his cabin. He passed out and slept the clock round. Barry had a black eye.

'It was only a game!' I protested. 'So he lost by a few points. What's the big deal?'

'He was living the part, Dodos. For someone who reads such a lot, you understand very little,' Greta said.

'He didn't just lose, Dee. He lost every single night,' Barry explained as if taking trouble to point out the obvious to a dim student.

And I've lost now. Not just for this night but for always.

Now that Barry was no longer mine, I couldn't stop thinking about him. His music: tin whistle, violin, piano. He could move from one to the other, swiftly transforming a wet evening in the apartment into a celebration. The way his hair curled at the back of his neck. How his hand held a hammer as he banged a nail into a wall. His pancakes that always stuck to the pan. The way he folded clothes as they came out of the dryer. I could dawdle over these routine affections as I rocked myself into a stupor but I would not let myself think of physical intimacies. The thoughts that I would never make love to him again filled me with despair.

Mrs Harty registered the change in atmosphere almost immediately.

'Something's wrong. You're all far too polite to each other. It's not natural,' she looked about her as if the answer was to be found in the kitchen.

'Being polite is meant to be natural, Gran. That's what Mom says when we're rude,' Cáit says for our instruction.

The Voiceover dropped them back in time for supper. He sits on Greta's right and Barry is on her left. I'm struck by how similar they are. Both tall, blond and talkative. They have monopolised the conversation throughout supper. Greta sits between them, playing ex-wife and current lover with a lightness that's becoming. I didn't want to feature in this little farce but Mrs Harty wouldn't take no for an answer. She has a way of bludgeoning me with concern that wears me down in no time. 'Back to the old US of A, the day after tomorrow,' Brian says, 'and my little darlings will be far away from their Daddy for another while.'

'We'll send you tapes as usual, Daddy,' Róisín says in

an auntly fashion as if to minimise his distress.

'I don't want to go back,' Cáit insists. 'I want to stay with Daddy for another while.'

'The tickets are booked,' Greta says. Her voice is restrained and firm.

'Daddy will be on location in Australia next week,' Róisín says, 'so there's no point in your staying. He wouldn't be here. Is it really a filthy movie, Daddy?'

'Who said anything about filth?' Brian is annoyed.

'Miss Brady in the post office. She read about it in the newspaper. She said it's full of naked bodies.'

'That's news to me but I'll keep her informed. I'll get a large fee. Enough for something special for both of you.'

'Enough for a pony?'

'We'll see. I don't like to make promises I can't keep.'

Mrs Harty laughs but tries to cover up by pretending to cough.

'I want to go to Australia. I like kangaroos.' Cáit smiles as if this logic will secure her the trip.

'Maybe next time round,' Brian soothes. 'You'll be bigger then.'

'And you'll be fatter,' she retorts.

'I have put on a pound or two since *Saffron* finished. I had to be so thin for the part that gluttony won through at the end of the run. I need to be fat for this film role.'

'But not bald,' Greta adds. 'Your hair grew back very quickly after *Saffron*.'

She runs her fingers through the blond spikes on his crown. He's pleased by this attention. Barry isn't. I can tell by the very precise way he's holding his spoon. Amazing the amount of stuff you know about someone when you've lived with them for a long time. Greta's eyes meet mine momentarily but I puncture my poached egg with a fork. I trail its golden lines about my plate.

'You're making a mess!' Cáit is gleeful.

'I like messes . . .' I say, '. . . some messes anyway,' I add.

'How was London?' Brian enquires.

'Busy. I shopped, ate out. That type of thing.'

'No theatre?'

'Tara and Geraldine aren't keen on drama and it was a kind of reunion spree.'

I'm crying. No warning. No sound. Just tears flowing. The children are alarmed.

'Mom. Dee is crying. Is it because she didn't go to the theatre?'

'This constant sunshine has everybody in a heap. A touch of sunstroke, that's what I'd say it is. I'll make a compress for your head, Deirdre. You probably spent too much time on that old swing with Lally,' Mrs Harty is burbling.

The Voiceover puts his arm around me and leads me from the kitchen to the drawing room. I don't remember him standing up and coming towards me. It's really dark in there. Mrs Harty keeps the curtains half drawn 'to keep the sun from fading every bit of upholstery. Sure the curtains have fine thick linings on them.'

I'm sitting on an overstuffed chaise longue, the faded peacocks of its fabric not even squeaking when I sit. He lifts my feet up. I'm a lady with the vapours forced to recline until I have recovered myself. 'I didn't mean to upset you.'

'It's not you.'

'Oh,' he says as if everything is now clear and he sits in silence. My tears flow on but I feel calm. I shouldn't have come down to supper. Sometimes the heart can't handle what the head accepts.

'It's Greta,' I say eventually, 'and Barry.'

'I know,' his voice is careful. Bedside manner. Don't rush the patient.

'How do you know?' I'm indignant.

'The way she patted his chair when they brought the kids to Midleton.'

We both laugh, then whisper like conspirators.

'It's one thing knowing it, but it's different when somebody else says it. Final somehow. No room for denials,' I'm brusque now, taking charge of myself again.

'People talk too much and too little about love,' he says. 'It's all mess in the end no matter what.'

His eyes rake the bookshelves when he speaks as if he urgently needs a particular book. I realise he's embarrassed.

'It's too difficult loving only one person in a lifetime but somehow when it gets to be more than one it becomes very exhausting. And confusing. I still love Greta but we weren't cut out for each other.'

'But you ran off with Penny!'

'Only for a week. Then Greta threw me out. Had to, I suppose. Her pride was hurt.'

'She was six months pregnant, for heaven's sake, and Róisín was only a toddler.'

'Exactly. She should have waited until Cáit was born. Instead she threw the best dinner set at the kitchen wall and gave my favourite clothes to a thrift store. I was walking down Forty Second Street the following week and I saw this guy coming towards me wearing my clothes. It was a shock.'

'Tough, tough!' My sympathy is staccato.

'So what's she going to do with this baby?'

His question fills the room. It seems like all the furniture has multiplied and there's no space for my eyes to rest on. I close them. Little patterns whirl behind my lids and I open them again.

'What baby?' I rasp.

'I thought you knew. I never know when to keep my mouth shut.'

'Nobody said anything about a baby,' I lean back fully on the cushions.

These past two weeks both Barry and Greta had been telling me to get my life in order. A baby! When had this happened? And where? In Greta's apartment, in the vast four poster bed? Or in our apartment in Spring Street?

Although I accepted the news that Brian had unwittingly divulged, the place of conception preoccupied me. Had this baby been conceived in our apartment?

Our apartment was a compromise between early American and Irish country house. Quaint is what acquaintances called it. Downright uncomfortable but impressive to look at is what friends agreed on. Austere Windsor chairs stood on duty next to a large pine dresser overflowing with Pender pottery. Overstuffed chintzy chairs were topped by antimacassars hemmed in Pender lace. A heavy-weight three legged black pot stood in the fireplace where a fire had never been lit. Barry lugged it back from Cork on a visit five years previously. Oak bookshelves held untidy collections of poetry, fiction, folklore and music. A baby grand piano took up half the study. Cupboards with glass doors held all sorts of instruments: tin whistles, bodhráns, fiddles, recorders, cymbals, prayer bells from India. Pressed flowers in heavy frames measured the length of the hallway: scilla hyacinthoides, lilium candidum, cyclamen persicum.

The answering machine was the only concession to late twentieth century convenience. That and the futon for visitors who stayed overnight. The kitchen had a double-sized gas cooker. No microwave made an appearance here.

'Goddamned convenience, my foot,' when I mentioned it might be useful, 'if it cooks that fast, there must be something nasty about it.'

Barry loved a bubbling pot and to be fair he provided most of the home-made food he thought wholesome and necessary: soups, casseroles, brown bread, all made from Mrs Harty's recipes. But mostly, because we were so busy, Frank's deli suited us perfectly. Our bedroom was a testimony to brownness. A sturdy oak bed with a rigid mattress dominated the room. This was flanked by a dressing table and tallboy in similar style. We shared one oversized bulky wardrobe, again of oak. You could stand upright inside this and still have room to sublet. Except this notion of space was erroneous the moment you hung clothes inside it. I had the right side of it and Barry the left. It looked roomy but it was always overflowing. The two doors swung open of their own accord no matter how many locksmiths we had in to look at it. The two enormous drawers at the end of it were curved. All part of the grand style but they often stuck and refused to move either way. I ended up storing most of my clothes in the airing cupboard and tallboy. But Barry wouldn't replace the wardrobe on any account. He had picked it up at an auction years ago and had lugged it about from one part of New York to another until he eventually settled into the Spring Street apartment.

The walls of the bedroom were lined with Barry's 'relatives,' paintings and photographs he'd bought from junk shops since he was a teenager. There was Grand Uncle Will, a be-whiskered New Englander, Aunt Eudora who managed to look forbidding even under a summer straw hat, Uncle Felix, the dapper alcoholic sporting a gold cane and a nineteen thirties Hitler moustache. Mama and Papa had been picked with extra care. She was plump but not overflowing, corsetted to decent proportions in a white suit. Her dark hair was bunned but not severely and there was a hint of secrecy about the rosebud smile. Papa was a business man. Waistcoated and suited. Hatless, he had looked fearlessly at the photographer, his grey eyes and greyer hair telling him he'd brook no nonsense. He was already late for a business appointment.

Is this where conception had taken place? In full view of Barry's carefully fabricated past! The Spring Street apartment was his creation. I added details on Barry's insistence, Pender pottery and lace. Apart from my shelves of poetry and fiction it was Barry's lair. His real mother had made her living on 42nd Street until her looks faded. His father, a tall handsome Swede, was her pimp.

Barry was raised in low rent apartments and low life hotels. He was sent to the movies when clients called.

When there was no money for movies, he was shoved on to the streets. He could easily have been absorbed by neighbourhood gangs but he was timid by nature. He preferred the dark movie theatres and big screen fantasies.

He discovered his musical talent by accident. One of his mother's clients left a guitar in the apartment. Barry started strumming it, taught himself a few songs. A teacher put him into the school band and a whole new life started. Music. Something for himself. Something separate from the sleaze of his home life. He was called after his mother's Irish grandfather. His parents never married. What pimp marries one of the girls from his stable? He had music and his Irishness to hold on to. He joined an Irish club and learned the tin whistle, fiddle and bodhrán. He became part of a cultural community for the first time in his life. He was fourteen years old and it saved him.

It saved him but it also made him duplicitous. Most of the people in the club came from closely knit Catholic families. He couldn't tell them his mother was a tart and his father a pimp. So he lied. He said both his parents were dead. They had been killed in an automobile accident when he was seven. He was living with an aunt on West 44th Street and Ninth Avenue. She was the caretaker of an apartment block. That's when he started buying up junk store relatives. Also, he began a photo album. Later he graduated to full scale portraits in gilt frames. Later still, I became a feather in his cap, genuine Irish, *déanta in Éirinn*.

He had wanted marriage almost since we met but I balked at such a commitment. Somehow I felt marriage would debilitate me, hem me in. Memories of Mam in her sick bed intruded. I would be weakened by the legalities of marriage. I said no, over and over until he believed me.

He wanted security. I wanted the freedom of ambiguity. And now Greta and Barry were going to provide enough ambiguity to last a very long time. Maybe the slur on my Irishness had unhinged him just as it had invigorated me.

Or was it the baby? Not this baby, Greta and Barry's. Our baby, Barry's and mine. My not having it? Was that what made the difference? Was that why he slept with Greta? For a baby? Who could hope to untangle all of this now?

At this very moment I feel I must have been crazy to entertain notions that I was Hungarian. For months, that's what I've wanted to be. Right now I'm equally convinced that Marge and Sam are right. There is no real evidence to go on. A literary concoction? It's almost as if Greta's claiming Barry has made me realise that this is where I belong. Not in the flat lands of the Hungarian plains or the high rise lakotelep of Budapest. I want to undo it all, proclaim myself a woman temporarily insane. One who has now regained sanity and new wisdom. Sackcloth and ashes. Would that do it? No. You can't overlook babies.

Forty-eight hours to go before all three of us were due to leave for New York. Were they waiting until then to tell me the news. What did Greta really feel?

The Voiceover was getting restless. His stare into the middle distance had reached a fixedness that one associates with unhappy daymares. Actors can only tolerate stage silences. It gives them something to react against. Real life silences they find intolerable.

'You've been very kind,' I say as I swing my feet to the ground once more and stand up.

'I've been stupid and hasty, you mean.'

'Right but also wrong. I don't think I really wanted to go back to New York just now. You've helped me decide to cancel my ticket, that's all. Barry and Greta did the rest.'

'You mustn't be vindictive or sour. It'll eat away at you if you let it. She's always been spontaneous.'

He wants me to forgive Greta! I've heard it all now. They drown you in a dark well and you're not meant to be disturbed by depth. He wants me to be the kind water diviner, to hold back from becoming the dark spirit of drought. I who have emptied and scraped my womb bare, how could I dance at a christening?

'Your ex-wife, my childhood friend, has become pregnant by my lover and you want me to bear in mind her spontaneity! If that's the way everyone feels about it, why hasn't anyone told me? Ms Piggy in the Middle, that's me.'

I go to the door and fling it open. I remember Miss Bateman's lessons and I open my mouth. I declaim in the direction of the open kitchen door.

'Greta and Barry, I'm amazed to hear you're going to have a baby. I wish either or both of you could have told me. In the light of this news I think it best that I stay here for another while.'

My own spontaneity vented in spite, I'm immediately sorry as I move towards the kitchen and I see Mrs Harty slowly lower herself into her rocking chair. Cáit and Róisín are no longer in the kitchen. I hope they haven't heard. I'd completely forgotten that they were here. Barry mumbles.

'We were going to tell you, Dee.'
'When? At the christening?'
Greta turns to her mother, 'It's not as bad as you think, Ma.'
Mrs Harty puts her hands over her ears, 'I don't want to hear anymore of this. I've heard enough. As soon as a girl forgets her religion, then there's trouble on the way. Harty and I did the best we could. We never expected any of this.'
'It'll sort itself out,' Brian offers a line from his last soap opera.
Mrs Harty rounds on him.
'Don't say anything, Brian. If you had kept promises you made at the altar instead of running off with that Penny woman that time, you'd still be married. None of this would have happened. Marriage is a sacrament. Anyone who makes little of it makes little of themselves.'
'We're going to get married, Ma,' Greta is gushing breathily in that little girl voice she uses on stage sometimes.
Barry drops his eyes to avoid looking at me.
'Sacred Heart of Jesus! When is the torment going to end? Marriage. You don't know the meaning of the word forever. So how can marriage make it alright? And what about Deirdre? Have either of you thought about her in all of this?'
All eyes are focused on me.
'I think I'll stay here for a while. In fact, I'll probably take a sabbatical. I don't want to be involved in wedding bells and baby talk.'
'I understand,' Greta says.
Greta is too willing to understand everything. Just as

long as she gets her way, of course. She smiles. That placatory childhood smile, the one she used so often when she'd outmanoeuvred me or pinched me without being detected. I smile too in spite of myself. My mind's eye roves over every little detail of the Spring Street apartment and I wonder if Greta's restless energy for decorating her cave will finally meet an immoveable obstacle.

* * *

They've gone. Greta left a note.

> *Dee,*
> *There is no excuse for what I've done. Pointless to say I'm sorry when I'm not. You went away. We did what we did. We tried to tell you when we arrived but it seemed impossible to say it in 'Field End'. You have a right to hate me.*
> *Greta.*

Forthright and plain. No frills. Greta accepted all blame. But I found it difficult to admire such straight talking this time round. Her words were nailed like horseshoes to the tacking room of my brain, inescapably and painfully in place.

Mrs Harty is scrubbing pots at the kitchen sink. As she scrubs, she talks. The pots weren't even dirty. She's doing it 'to calm her nerves' as she puts it. It's still quite early. Only about half past eight but it seems like I've already been up for days. They left here at half past six this morning. They had an early flight. I said goodbye to all of them last night. Greta and Barry took the girls on daytrips these past two days. Just as well. I didn't enquire where they went and only pretended to listen when Cáit and Róisín told me the details of their days when they returned. I watched them setting out and returning home. I peeped out through the lace curtains in Mam's sewing room. Two adults, two children, a family on a day's outing. Hatred surfaced and I didn't know what to do with it. Pointless to ask either of them anything now.

I walked a lot these last two days. To Giant's Stone, to the village and beyond. August 31st. I should be at college at the first faculty meeting of the year. Mrs Harty covered Tim's and Lally's schoolbooks in brown paper last night in preparation for their new school year. What will I do with this sabbatical yawning in front of me?

'I could never understand Greta, not even as a tiny child. She was wilful then too. There was no way that Harty and I could persuade her not to do something if her mind was set on it. Do you remember that time she jumped from the stable roof? Her leg was in plaster for weeks after that.'

I remember it clearly. Greta, her left leg in plaster, smirked at me from her hospital bed.

'Well, what are you looking at, Dodos! Say something.'

'I . . . I . . . Why . . . why did you jump?'

'Never mind why. I missed school, didn't I? Want to autograph my cast?'

'Well, she never did tell us why she jumped from that stable roof. Not to this day,' Mrs Harty puts the last saucepan in the cupboard. 'But this latest news tops the lot. I can't bring myself to tell Harty about it just yet. And how the two of them could do that to you and have the cheek to come here on holiday is beyond me. Maybe you won't want me around the place after this? I am Greta's mother after all. She's convinced you'll probably sell out anyway.' She sits into her rocking chair.

'Greta's wrong. I'm not going to sell.'

Greta presumes too much. After the baby business I was going to saddle up and race into the night. Then I got to thinking, why the hell should I? This was my home after all. Home. The place I belonged to. I had turned my eyes elsewhere, away from 'Field End', since Mam and Dad's death. To Hungary because of Dad's journal. I had wanted mystery, intrigue, excitement, a chance to discover an alternative. But since Greta's announcement of marriage and motherhood, I had turned my eyes to home. Taken stock. Lisa was right. There was more to Dad's pages. An outline for a book maybe? Pages cut out from a newspaper and juxtaposed with events in his own life? They made sense on some level but not what my wild imaginings had conjured up. Old Dr Caird was a stickler for detail. He wouldn't have put his professional life on the line by taking part in a cloak and dagger melodrama. And besides hadn't I listened more than once to Mrs Harty's colourful version of my arrival.

'You nearly killed your mother, you did. Twenty-six hours labour. And such a tiny thing when you arrived after all of that. Up there in the yellow room and not even a moan out of her. And Mr Pender had a track worn on the landing. Too nervous to smoke even.'

Home meant more than stutters and silences. It was Dad reading *Alice in Wonderland* aloud, sharing the swing with Greta, taking Sandysocks out in early morning knowing I was the first up. Racing to the Giant's Stone with Marge and Sam. Mam hadn't meant her clever hands to pull on me like a weight. She sewed love into those dresses. That the beauty of her creations made me feel inadequate must have been a lack in me. Not to stand out, that's all I wanted as a child. Her illnesses and the clothes she made for me made that impossible in such a small village.

'Are you sure you won't be sellin'?' Mrs Harty is doubly cautious.

'Of course I am,' I reply briskly, a petulant child, crossed. Can't blame the woman really. From her point of view I'm not exactly the solid-as-a-rock type. After all, I chopped off my hair, said I wasn't my parents' child, broke crockery, retired to the nursery, spent weeks in Limerick and 'London' without leaving her an address. Since then I've spent days on the orchard swing with Lally, refusing to budge even for daytrips to the sea.

'I know I haven't behaved very well, Mrs Harty.'

'When my own mother died, I couldn't sleep for months. I'd Harty persecuted. He'd be up makin' tea for me in the middle of the night. A man that needed to rest that back of his. But I couldn't settle my mind, couldn't sleep. Didn't see the point in her death, knocked down crossing a zebra crossing.'

'I remember her funeral. Greta fainted when they started shovelling in the earth.'

'Drawin' attention to herself like that. I was mortified. Not to talk about what she said when she came to. The boldness of it all.'

'She said Mam should have died instead of her Gran. She called Mam a bloody creakin' door that would go on forever. Nobody said anything about the zebra crossing. We thought she died in her sleep. From her bad cough.'

'It was hushed up because of the canon.'

'Canon Burke?'

'No, a strange canon. A Dublin man. He knocked her down. The hospital kept her in for two weeks and she seemed fine when she came home but she died three months later. Harty said the canon killed her and he was right.'

'But what about the death cert?'

'Natural causes, it said, but what's natural about the shock you'd get after been knocked down on a zebra crossing?'

'I've never heard a cough like hers since,' I say.

'Poor Mammy. Smoker's cough. Loved her cigarettes she did. It used to drive Harty crazy seein' her with the cigarette in the side of her mouth, sittin' by the fire surrounded by the children. Babysat for me every Saturday night while myself and Harty went to the pictures. I never took much pleasure in the films after her death. Greta wet the bed for a long time after that. She was very attached to her Gran.'

'Greta never told me about the bed-wetting,' I protest.

'Knew when to keep her mouth shut even then, but this latest escapade takes the biscuit. Stealin' Barry from under your nose.'

'I wasn't there.'

'Well, behind your back then. Do you think it's something to do with the bees?' It's a genuine inquiry but as far as I'm concerned it's a non-sequitor. I'm confused.

'We haven't had hives for years, not since the fire.'

'Not bees! The letter B. There was Brian, then Ben and now Barry. They all begin with B and in the end Brian and Ben left her.'

'Barry will stick with Greta,' I assure her. 'He's a man of fixed habits. He doesn't like change and he loves children.'

'If he's slow to change then why did he leave you after seven years? I never thought it was right, the two of you livin' in sin but I felt sure ye'd tie the knot in the end. And now that hussy of mine has grabbed him for herself.'

'Things were never the same after the . . .' I stop myself just in time, 'Barry and me, we were into a routine and it suited us both for a time but we're very different in lots of ways. I still love him. You can't stop loving someone overnight. I feel betrayed by both of them.'

'It's the poor baby stuck in the middle that's worrying me. Nobody asks to be born. Greta will come a cropper some day yet. Too much cheek, that's her problem. Always was. Do you know what she said to me the other night in my own kitchen and Harty only a stone's throw away in the garden shed, "We both wanted the baby, Ma." Just like that, bold as you please. Like a child takin' sweets without permission.'

A picture of Greta and Barry, heads bent in concentration over a baby name book in the study in Spring Street has ballooned inside my head as if it's actually happening at this precise moment. Mrs Harty offers me a tissue.

'What can I be thinking of? Blatherin' on like that, addin' to your misery!'

*   *   *

Greta's news has catapulted me from the nursery. I left it the very night of the Voiceover's disclosure. My one-eyed teddy with his snub nose and Rockabye with his sleek wood seemed to mock me. I left everything behind except Dad's journal. Which room to go to? I assumed Greta and Barry were in the large double blue room, the one Aunt Em and Alice favoured during my childhood. I wondered what they thought of the room's inmates now as I tiptoed past at three in the morning, Dad's journal in my hand, a blanket trailing me. Would Alice and Em's genteel ghosts rise up to spook them in the night? Greta called the blue room the 'Alem Suite,' a compression neither of them would have appreciated. Cáit and Róisín were in the pink room three doors down from their mother. The expected arrival of a new half-sibling was unknown to them. They had been in the orchard with Lally at the time of my declamatory revelation. 'I'll tell them on home ground, Ma,' Greta had said when pushed about her intentions.

Home ground. Nearly everyone had some sense of that except for the homeless. For the first time since my return I began to think of myself as fortunate. I might be roaming the corridors at three in the morning wondering what room to sleep in — not to mention the fact that my best friend was in the same bed as my lover. But I still had choice. Rooms to move into and out of. An academic post that had given me the freedom of a sabbatical.

When I moved to New York a decade before, the

sight that shocked me most was the Port Authority Bus Terminal at 42nd Street. A home for the homeless. Down and outs, they lived there and harassed bona fide travellers who queued for buses. I found it difficult to accept such poverty only blocks from enormous wealth. Later when I met Barry and he told me that he played there as a child, I understood the 'family portraits' on the walls in Spring Street. Not to mention the fastidious care with which he'd assembled the photo albums. Every year in 'his' life was chronicled in these. The black and white phase ended in 'his' 14th year. A youth remarkably like Barry posed holding a cup for first prize in the swimming team. After that, colour photos and his developing musicianship progressed into real pictures.

Barry with tin whistle, Barry playing the fiddle, Barry, right hand in mid air ready to hit a bodhrán. On and on these photo albums went. One for each year right up to the present. Barry at the SoHo Centre for visual artists with a glass of wine in his hand. Barry and Deirdre on the beach at Cape Cod last year. The photo albums are a reminder to Barry of the distance he's travelled from the Port Authority Bus Terminal to Spring Street.

And is this home for me? 'Field End?' I ask myself as I tread carefully to avoid the creaky board outside the blue room at three in the morning. What about the Hungarian connection? The first apartment I shared with Greta and Brian when I moved to New York, our neighbour was Hungarian. She was a little old lady, quite diminutive, under five feet. She had Nepszava, the Hungarian newspaper, delivered weekly. Her apartment was the smallest in the building, one room.

Belonging

Yet she had a constant stream of visitors, quite a few who stayed overnight. People with one suitcase and little English. Greta was kind to her, picked up her groceries and alerted her to any bargains in the supermarket every week.

'She sleeps on a day-bed. One of those fold-up chairs. She's got two couches and a stove and she's happy. Makes me wonder why the hell I'm dissatisfied. Hey, Voiceover, squeeze your pregnant spouse a fresh juice. This play is driving me nuts. The writer is on stage every day sparring with the director. They call it communication. In this heat and this pregnant, I call it harassment.'

Brian squeezed mountains of oranges throughout Greta's first pregnancy. They were happy and I was glad to be with people I knew until I got my bearings in New York. At first, I'd said I couldn't possibly intrude but they insisted they'd be relieved to share the rent particularly with all the expense of a first baby looming. The second baby was on its way faster than either of them planned and it was during Greta's second pregnancy that the Voiceover ran off with Penny.

Aeons ago now. Sometimes when I'd get home from graduate school Zelda, the babyminder, would be there with the kids. I'd help her bathe them and get them to bed, sending them to sleep with the same story again and again, *The Pig Who Had No Tail*. They loved it. Afterwards we would sit in the yellow kitchen waiting for the popcorn to pop in the glass saucepan. 'Better than watching TV,' she'd say. Pop, pop, pop. While the corn cooled we'd put the living room to rights. Zelda was Austrian. She came to New York in the forties with her parents. Her English was splendid but she said, 'I refuse to speak American' and so she spoke in halting aristocratic English that pleased her but upset her relatives.

'Wake up, Zelda. New York is home. Vienna is in the past, forget it,' her brother said over and over. But she told him, 'New York is where I live but Vienna is where I belong.'

She loved children, had six of her own. All of them had left home by the time I met her at Greta's.

'I luff children. Adults are so dull,' was one of her favourite sayings.

And now she's left the neighbourhood, left the country. Gone. Not to Vienna but to Canada. Willowdale Ontario, to live with one of her daughters and her children. I wonder does she still think that Vienna is where she belongs. Barry had taken her place as babysitter to Cáit and Róisín. And Greta has taken my place in Barry's bed. They feel they belong to each other now. They're heading into parenthood so maybe they do. Hapless or brave? Who knows? I couldn't be hemmed in by motherhood last year. The changes it would have demanded were beyond me. Feelings were never completely right between Barry and me after that. We pretended and relied on time to change things again. But that didn't happen.

In a curious dual consciousness, while I stood outside their bedroom door I hoped their leap into parenthood would work. I summoned a winged horse to bear them skyward. This did not alleviate in the least my own outrage and anger with them. As I moved forward down the corridor, my steps tread a series of creaking boards. I didn't care if they knew I was prowling in the dead of night.

I eventually came to a standstill outside Mam's sewing room. I passed through this to the sleeping room and it is here, in these two rooms, that I have set myself up. I threw myself on the bed, crawled under the blanket I'd brought from the nursery and fell asleep. Since then, much to my surprise, I've really settled in. I've left her Singer sewing machine on the table by the window but I've removed its cover. September sunlight picks out its gold and black. Lally works at it some evenings.

'It's like the ones in our history books,' she says.

I've made the sewing room my study. Barry sent my books and college files. Now they occupy the three wall-high pine bookshelves I bought at Finerty's Furniture shop. I moved the St Gertrude statue into the pantry but I've decorated the other walls by framing six pieces of Mam's lacework. The sleeping room I've changed a little. I think of it now as my bedroom. The faded green and gold of the wallpaper's pattern is a subdued background for the violently coloured holy pictures of Mary, the Sacred Heart and Don Bosco. I add a neo-expressionist painting I bought at Mary Boone's gallery on West Broadway. Its rich palette is not disturbed by the saints.

A lot has happened in the last six weeks since Greta and Barry went back to New York. I didn't fly back to Budapest. A flat in Vatci Utca on the same floor as Katya's, Lisa's translator, became free. But after Greta's baby news I felt incapable of leaving 'Field End'. Before that when I had thought about a sabbatical I felt propelled towards Budapest. In a curious way Greta and Barry's baby changed this impulse to its reverse.

Before I knew about their baby, I wanted to be Inga's daughter. Now, I hoped I wasn't. In fact I was beginning to entertain Marge's view that the journal was indeed some of the debris of Dad's literary endeavours.

Lisa, an objective assessor of all this family trauma, was inclined to agree with the literary theory. After all, I had failed to come up with anything concrete except that Inga Kadir had travelled to Canada in 1957. I postponed my return to Budapest indefinitely. Lisa left the Hilton and took the flat in Vatci Utca. She wrote saying how much she enjoyed its bustle. Living in a pedestrian shopping street she could watch the window shoppers late at night and also she was now within walking distance of Gerbeaud's. A serious consideration for a devoted pastry fiend, she assured me. She disapproved of the MacDonalds that had opened up on a street just off Vatci Utca. It now had queues longer than those outside the Adidas shop.

Greta's certainty that I would sell 'Field End' fuelled my obstinacy. A new routine had established itself since my flight from the nursery. Mrs Harty was delighted to see me installed in 'Mrs Pender's quarters' as she called them. Banishing St Gertrude to the pantry had given her a 'queer start' though. Then I reminded her of all those St Gertrude high teas she had made over the years and said the pantry was a perfect place for Gertrude, now that Mam was no longer here. That mollified her, particularly when I said I had no intention of moving the pictures of Mary, the Sacred Heart and Don Bosco.

When I had arranged my books on the shelves and hung Mam's framed lace pieces on the wall, I called the room my study. Mrs Harty approved fully of my 'rehabilitation'. That's the exact word I heard her use to Marge. They were at the herb patch. I was hidden from their view as I picked blackberries with Lally in the adjoining field.

'Rehabilitation, no other word for it, Marge. I think it's her Mam prayin' up there for her,' she stopped momentarily. They both looked at three cumulus clouds in the sky as if Mam was perched there.

She continued, 'She was behavin' like a madwoman over this Hungarian business, cuttin' off her hair and talkin' to teddies in the nursery. Then our Greta comes home with Barry and drops a real clanger and there's no more talk about Hungary.'

'A form of denial. Hysteria is often a common reaction to grief. Dee has had a sheltered life in many ways. Still, she seems normal enough these days, thank goodness.'

'I always think it's tougher on only children when parents die. They've no brothers and sisters to argue with, you see. Harty and myself dealt with that one. There'll be ten of them to scream and roar when we're gone.'

'Death is difficult to deal with, no matter when it happens.'

'Work and routine. They're the best ingredients to get over any sorrow. You can't beat routine for keepin' people goin'. Dee is into a routine now and that will keep her goin'. Breakfast at eight every morning. Goes off to her study until twelve, out for a walk until one, lunch, then back in there until four. All that readin' and writin'. I can't see the sense in it myself but she says she's writin' a book. At least she's not mopin'.'

'She should get out and about more. Tom and I try to include her in things but it's not easy.'

'It's not easy for anyone these days. I was worried there for a while that the place would be up for sale and I'd be stuck in the cottage with Harty from mornin' till night. It wouldn't have suited either of us. We both like our bit of freedom.'

For years I've wanted to write a book on Emily Dickinson's poetry but never had the time. Now I'm happily dug in with my research books and my own thoughts about the poems from early morning to late afternoon. I'm finding it difficult but wonderful. I'm able to work very well in my study. It's as if the years of Mam's stitchery is casting a benign aura and my hands race over the typewriter keys at an impressive pace. I've bought a car, a mini. I call it Emily for luck. I see Marge once a week for lunch. We've become friendly again now that Africa has reclaimed Sam once more. I prefer to see her on her own without Tom or the kids. She has hidden her girlishness now that Sam's not here and become wife and matron once more. Her appetite has diminished and I notice lines around her eyes and mouth that I'm sure weren't there a few weeks ago.

Now that I'm into a routine, she's more willing to listen to my vagaries from time to time. She admired the way I'd framed Mam's work. She's decided to start a small museum at the lace factory. This will exhibit different styles from 1750 to the present. There will be a Sarah O'Brien Pender section. She wants me to select the ones I'd like. I'm happy. We pick out several of Mam's pieces and then change our minds completely. I lay them out on my bed. The final choice isn't made yet. Glad to be cousins again, maybe, we're postponing this, prolonging the task. It shapes our conversations.

I haven't turned my back completely on Limerick and Hungary. I keep the four parts of Dad's journal on a side table in the study: the blue-inked copybook in English, the black-inked one in Hungarian, the homemade photo album and finally the book of newspaper cuttings from the fifties. Next to these I place Katya's single page translation. Mam used this table to hold scraps of material. When I was a child I remember arranging and re-arranging Mam's scraps. She might have been in bed sewing or sitting out on the terrace just off her room. I made houses, stables, friends of these patches. Now I try to make sense of Dad's scrappy journal.

Each day I work on my book. I put Greta and Barry from my mind but sometimes they intrude. New York memories crowd my head at unexpected moments. Evenings of music at the Irish Arts Centre on West 51st Street. There were a lot of those. Barry was one of the people who helped the centre develop from a single music class held in a bar to the thriving centre it is today. I didn't go there as often as Barry but I'd drop in once a week, usually on Thursday evenings. Monday nights were usually spent in the Broome Street Bar. We'd have three Rolling Rock beers, a hamburger and a gooey dessert. Musicians ate there, and Barry knew most of the regulars, so we'd join a group of them at some stage in the evening and talk music. I miss girly chats with Greta: sharing the mutual rage at premenstrual tension or buying half-bottles of champagne when we were almost broke. Other things too — I always helped her shred her worst reviews. She'd pile them up on her kitchen shelves for six months or so, then she'd ring me.

'You want to help me shred some reviews on Saturday?'

'Okay, what time?'

'Nine thirty. The kids will be in bed by then. Bring some eats. I'll supply the whiskey.'

And I'd pick up a giant pizza and a bucket of Haagen-Dazs ice cream, chocolate with almonds, our favourite, and we'd shred, and talk and eat and drink until the small hours. We'd set fire to the reviews in a metal trash can and Greta would toast their demise,

'All my enemies in flames. Death to the arid bastards! Destroyers, not creators. Death to all of you.'

Does Barry celebrate their burning with her now? I want to feel remote from such primitive jealousy but I can't. I work feverishly by day and usually manage to centre my mind on the work but at night, in my celibate bed, I torture myself with their imagined couplings.

I have sent Irina, my Head of Department, an outline of the first chapter of my book.

* * *

I'm reassured by her response to it. Irina doesn't waste words. She writes,

Dear Dee,
A very good start if you don't make the mistake of
intruding research in the wrong places. Your replacement,
a Czechoslovakian woman called Anna (specialises in
Modern European Poetry) is competent. She has engaged

*some big names for readings next semester, terrific for the
Dept. Faculty meetings are restful without you. We look
forward to your return but only if you finish the book on
time. Writers write, teachers teach. I do remind my staff of
this from time to time but some of them are too lazy to fit
their writing into vacation time. You won't make that
mistake though, will you?
Irina.*

I planned to go to Limerick last week but never got there. The night before I had been cleaning out the blue room, the 'Alem suite', and I came across a book of pressed flowers. On one page there was a precise drawing of a specimen and on the facing page was the pressed flower. I turned the pages on bog asphodel, bog pimpernel, fringed water lily and crinkle-leaved pond weed. Underneath the drawing of the water lily a handwritten note said, picked by Hattie. Hattie? Who was she? Then I remembered and blushed my embarrassment into the musty leaves of the book. Hattie. One of Alice and Em's gentlewomen. Hattie who was a decade older than both of them and had outlived them. She had taken her place in church at Mam and Dad's funeral with that decisive frailty that the very old have. I hadn't bothered to talk to her afterwards. I ask Mrs Harty where she lives now.

'She's in the same flat in Nash Lodge as she's always been. What do you want her for?'

'I'm sorry I didn't speak to her after the funeral,' I say lamely.

'Nothing to reproach yourself with, Deirdre. You were in no fit state to communicate with any Christian on that day. Your Mam and Dad always had Hattie to tea on St Stephen's Day. Boxing Day, she called it, of course. She's well looked after where she is.'

'These are some of her pressed flowers. I found them in the blue room last night.'

'At the rate you're clearing out rooms it'll be next summer before you get to the end of it.'

I had been clearing out rooms over the past few weeks. I started with the nursery. At first Mrs Harty was very upset. She took it as a criticism of her work. Then I told her it was a kind of therapy, to sort me out and settle me in. She said she understood or at least she pretended she did. I did this work for an hour or two in the evening after I had a walk or a visit to the village.

I got heavy brown cardboard boxes to store things in the attic. The work was as slow as Mrs Harty said because I found so much of interest to look at. Things that I hadn't thought about or really noticed about the place for years now took on an overwhelming significance. In Dad's glass collection I found the plain marbles he bought me once. We used to play, Dad, Mam and I on the terrace in summer evenings. Not talking much, the marbles bumping together, no colour to distract our attention, our eyes focused on shape alone. These shapes I now hold in my hand. A dozen of them. I keep them in a jar on my desk. I can look at them as I write. When it came to sorting out their wardrobes, every coat, blouse and shirt looked so much in place that it seemed impossible that they should hang anywhere else. I opened the door and Dad's greenhouse jacket swung out at me. It smelt of tomatoes and tobacco. Mam's blouses. Dozens of them in creams and whites looked as crisp as they'd always done. Careful people, my Mam and Dad.

How could I have wanted to turn my back on them? Mam and Dad who had never been intentionally cruel or neglectful of me. Whose love had cosseted me, thinking it for the best. It's pure chance the parents we get. Barry's father called once a week during his childhood to collect the major part of his mother's earnings. He beat her if they fell below his expectations. His mother had been pushed and pulled by hardships all her life until the bottle got her in the end. Barry felt locked out for most of his childhood until he discovered music. Music and his membership of the Irish community-twin badges. He wore them and he belonged. I had been given stability from the start but there were times when I felt as locked out as Barry. Did this make sense? How could I feel such anger against Mam and Dad? Wanting to be Hungarian as an explanation for that anger is melodramatic to say the least. Why had my brain and heart turned full circle when the Voiceover dropped the grenade — Greta's baby? Writing by day and cleaning the house systematically by night had persuaded me that this was my home, my place. But still I iconised the tatty journal.

I visited Hattie on my way to Limerick, except I never got to Limerick in the end. I had rung two days before to make the arrangement. She was pleased. Her voice crackled with age but also excitement.

'So glad you've decided to pop round. Been thinking I'd put my foot in it when you hadn't called.'

I parked 'Emily' outside Nash Lodge (home to eight distressed Protestant ladies by the grace of the will of Charlotte Nash who had lived and died here in the last century). The stone house had a severe appearance. No ivy greened its walls but shutters kept out cold in winter and the flats were large and cheerful. At least that was my memory of the place. I had accompanied Alice, my favourite aunt, on many visits here as a child. The old bell was gone, I noticed, as I pressed the intercom button. A sturdy voice, not Hattie's, answered.

'Yes. Whom do you wish to visit?'

The formality and precision of the question reduced me to a schoolgirl again.

'I'm Deirdre Pender. I'm visiting Hattie Carlton.'

I felt myself blush as I listened to my voice. I could be back in Sister Agnes's class again, stuttering my way through *I wandered lonely as a cloud*. A buzzer, then the door springs open and I'm inside. Time has stood still in the black and white tiled hallway. The enormous oak hall stand with nothing hanging from it is in its usual place. The portrait of Charlotte Nash above the white marble fireplace smiles on anyone looking her way. Now that my eyes have adjusted to the dim interior I see a glass window which appears to be part of an office. That's new. A large woman with close cut hair pulls the window across.

'Ms Pender. I'm Matron. Ms Carlton expects you. Number one is down the hallway first turn to your right.'

I nod and head in the direction of Hattie's room. I can feel Matron's eyes on me as I click my way down the hallway. Hattie has obviously heard my approach as she's standing in the doorway when I get there. Her white hair has the same strict cut as Matron's. She's wearing a pretty lavender suit with a white lace blouse.

Beige flat slip-on shoes can't disguise the dainty feet.

'I'm delighted you've called, Dee. You young people today have such busy lives. Computers,' she says as if this is self explanatory. 'You look well but you haven't grown?' It's a serious query.

'I'm thirty-two, Hattie. My growing days are over.'

'Really! Are you? Seems like only yesterday . . . still, at my age thirty-two is the toddler stage.'

'You're looking well,' and I look about the room.

'I'm very well, thank goodness, but I get slower and smaller. Every time I look in the mirror, I'm shorter. What did you do to your beautiful hair?'

'I could ask you the same question,' I banter.

'Matron likes things tidy. Hair, fires, snakes and ladders.'

'Snakes and ladders?'

'Do you remember the Juniper sisters, Peggy and Ba?'

'Course I do. They live here, don't they?'

'Yes, in number three but the stuffing's been knocked out of them.'

'But they're the youngest in the house, the most active.'

'Oh, they still swing golf clubs and play bridge but they won't open a box of snakes and ladders again.'

'Why?'

'Too rowdy, Matron says. Said she couldn't tolerate the arguments about cheating.'

'But they've always cheated,' I blurt out without thinking.

'Precisely,' Hattie affirms. 'They play to cheat and argue. Everyone understands that except Matron. She gave them such a telling off they both said they'd never play again. Dug themselves into a corner, you see. And Matron locked them up.'

'But that's against the law.'

'Is it really? They didn't get legal advice on the matter.'

'Denying them their freedom, that's dreadful.'

'No, not them, dear. She hasn't locked Peggy and Ba up. Good gracious, no. The board games. Locked them into the office. You can see it's knocked them for six but they're too proud to admit it. Anyway, enough tittle-tattle. Pull over to the fire and tell me all your news.'

The fire isn't lit but a basket filled with logs flanks its left side.

'That's another thing, we're not allowed fires in our rooms anymore. Too dangerous, matron says. Central heating day in, day out, except on Sundays when the fire is lit in the drawing room for dinner. I like to look at the logs even if I can't have a fire.'

Hattie falls silent, remembering maybe the spirit of past fires that lit her grate. The room has been newly papered in a dark heavy green wallpaper but little else seems changed. The fireplace, a high panelled one, is painted plain cream. Two black and gold vases filled with dried flowers stand at either end of the overmantel. In the centre is the wedding picture of her parents at the turn of the century. Around it are clustered baby pictures of her various charges, all surely middle-aged by now. A chintzy couch and two matching chairs are grouped about the fireplace.

A china cabinet filled to overflowing with china and glass stands to the right of the window. There are three free-standing lamps with lampshades of dusty pink marshalled at regular intervals about the room. They've been on duty for years. I've never been in Hattie's bedroom, the room off this one. Aunt Alice used to tease her that she had trunkloads of treasure in there. She enjoyed the fun.

'Nonsense,' Aunt Em interjected once, when Alice had been entertaining us with tales of Hattie's treasure during tea. 'She's as poor as the proverbial church mouse. Retired nannies live on memories and a miserly pension.'

I reach across to Hattie's chair and place the book of pressed flowers on its arm.

'I found it last night. I was clearing out the blue room. Thought you might like to have it.'

She's pleased and handles it shyly as if the young woman who picked and pressed these flowers had returned.

'Takes me back. Such fun your aunts were. Even Em. She liked to organise us. Wouldn't allow us take a walk without coming back with something.'

She turns the pages with concentrated care.

'I was keen on marsh and stream flowers then. Their wildness attracted me.'

Time is getting on. I want to ask questions but I don't want to intrude on her memories. After some minutes she closes the book firmly and looks at me directly. I'm startled by the intensity of her gaze.

'You've come to talk about something in particular.' Her eyes do not leave mine. I'm embarrassed, lower my gaze to the faded leaves of the ugly brown carpet on the floor.

'How did you know?'

'Experience, my dear. Can't beat it. I've put

generations of the Balcombe-Smythes through my hands. You develop a sixth sense for such things. They still come to visit now and then, mostly in times of crisis, a marriage ended, money lost. They come to tell Nanny hoping she can make it alright. I can't of course, but telling me takes some of the burden from them. Now, tell me why you've come.'

Her directness reminds me of Lisa's that night in Budapest when she told me that lives were simple affairs. 'It's Dad's journal. He left it with Fogarty for me.'

'And what's the problem. Can't you publish it? After years of work too. Em was always sceptical.'

'But they're just a jumble of old copybooks,' I protest.

'Yes. But so many of them. Too long, is that the problem? I thought the blockbuster was the thing these days.'

'There are only four copies and not much writing in any of them. In fact one is a jumble of newspaper cuttings and the other is a selection of photos.'

'You must have got his little notebook. He used a new copybook each month. That's what Sarah said. Wrote in them for years. Ever since that refugee business in Limerick in the fifties. That's what gave him the idea in the first place. Nobody read his work, not even Sarah. Time enough when I'm not around. Deirdre will look after it then. That's what he said.'

'But where have the copybooks gone?'

'When he finished one, he put it with the others in the greenhouse, in that cupboard with the fertilisers. He made no secret of that.'

'Are you sure about all this?'

Maybe Hattie is senile, but in a creative way not

detectable on the surface? Dad wrote in his study. I knew nothing about this greenhouse business.

"Course I am. Alice used to tease him about "something nasty in the greenhouse".'

I'm impatient to leave to see if the copybooks are still there but I've been back since May and it's mid September now. Each day I've puzzled over the cryptic components of the journal. I can wait a little longer and besides, Hattie may know something about the Hungarian connection.

'The parts of the journal Fogarty gave to me are confusing.' I make an effort to keep my voice steady. 'In fact, one time when I tried to piece together what was in them I thought that Mam and Dad weren't my parents at all. That I was the daughter of a Hungarian refugee, Inga, who came to Limerick in 1956.'

Hattie's laughter is energetic for one her age.

'My goodness! How even the simplest things can cause confusion. Your parents sent money and clothes for the refugees in Limerick. Your father was one of the official visitors. Even got himself a Hungarian dictionary to attempt the language. Your mother was expecting you at the time. She wasn't young and after so many miscarriages and of course, her other condition, she had to be careful. They wanted you so much, it was painful to watch.'

'But what had Inga to do with all of this?'

'She was a refugee. Got herself into trouble as they used to say back then. Her baby was due at around the same time as Sarah's. She took a special interest in her progress. You know how superstitious these Romans are.'

Romans? Now I'm lost.

'Romans?'

'I'm so sorry, my dear. I've forgotten my manners. Of course you're one of them too. We never really considered John one even after he'd converted.'

Comprehension at last.

'Roman Catholic?'

'Precisely. Sarah had been through so much that John rather indulged her little ways. She got it into her head that if they provided for Inga and her baby in their new life in Canada that her own baby would be born perfectly healthy. She was afraid you'd inherit her condition.'

'Epilepsy.'

'Yes, but of course you didn't. You were perfectly fine apart from the stammering but then Sarah was grand mal and as it turned out Miss Bateman did wonders.'

And I'd lived in a fog of inferiority all my early life, afraid to speak in case words wouldn't come, thinking there was something terribly wrong with me!

'Nobody explained any of this. You mean my stammering is connected with Mam's epilepsy?'

She nods.

'Things were done differently then, Deirdre. Your Aunt Em was of the opinion that Sarah's condition was best hushed up. She was terribly disappointed in John's marriage. Marrying outside his class and creed was a dreadful blow to her. She rather dominated the household, I'm afraid. She thought if you knew the truth about your mother that you'd become a nervous child. And she was kind-hearted in other ways. She wanted only what was best for you.'

The clock strikes eleven. Ping, ping, ping, eleven

times. A chime I remember from years ago. Hattie blinks.

'I'm tired my dear. I haven't talked so much in a long time, not since before dear Alice died.'

She rises stiffly.

'You must come again. I love to see young people.'

I pick up my bag and let myself out, having kissed Hattie on her old-baby cheek. I click my way back down the corridor and out the front door under the watchful eye of Matron. I turn 'Emily' in the direction of home instead of Limerick. I want to check out the greenhouse copybooks. Limerick can wait.

I am back at the house in ten minutes. It's a short drive. The drawing room piano is thonking discordantly. Mrs Harty's hand holds a yellow duster and runs up and down its keys. She's startled by my return.

'An accident? You're as white as a sheet.'

She expects my daily demise in the mini.

'No. Changed my mind about Limerick, that's all.'

'Better ring your friends then.'

'I already have,' I lie. 'Have you changed anything in the greenhouse lately?'

'Of course not. That's Tom Burke's territory . . . 'twas Mr Pender's favourite place after his study. Used to sit out there for hours puffing on that pipe of his.'

'What about the copybooks?'

'I never touched a thing,' she makes a swipe at the piano stool. Little puffs of dust rise. 'His own private business. He put them in that big box in the cupboard after he filled 'em up. Wrote in them one by one in his study, then put them in that box. Never touched a thing. Not my place.'

It's raining. A late September shower. I run out to the

greenhouse. Tom Burke is sitting on Dad's chair, the butt of a cigarette about to burn his fingers.

'Mornin', Dee. Thought you'd be in Limerick by now. Mrs Harty said you left early.'

'I didn't go. Changed my mind. I'm looking for Dad's copybooks. He kept them out here.' I point to the cupboard.

'That's right. Put them in there, he did.'

I pull the door open impatiently. Two brown cardboard boxes. Dusty but not too dusty. One full, the other three quarters full with copybooks. Even at a glance I can see that some of the covers are faded. I open the top one, rifle its pages impatiently. Every page is full. Not a line skipped or wasted. All written in the same blue ink. Quink, I presume. I remember the first time Dad let me fill his fountain pen. Greta couldn't understand my excitement. It was the night before I made my first communion. I was nervous about the following day and had spent the afternoon with Sandysocks — a long run, riding away the tension. Mam was taking a rest in her sleeping room. It was before dinner. I filled the pen from the Quink bottle. I was delighted at my own expertise. Aunt Em knocked on the study door and came in with bunches of white and purple lilac.

'I'm asphyxiated with these May altars, John,' she said briskly.

'Deirdre has filled my pen. Hasn't spilt a drop of ink either. Isn't she clever?'

And now, here were dozens of copybooks written with the same fountain pen. 'A good pen lasts a lifetime,' was one of his maxims and he disdained biros.

I'm impatient to read them. Tom helps me lift the boxes into my study. I emerge a few hours later, dazed. This is no novel, no great work of literature. It's a diary. Each copybook is divided in four, a week to each section. A new copy each month, twelve for each year. The first one starts in June 1937, the month he married Mam. The last one ends April 1989, the month he died.

Reading them fills me with remorse for my recent defection. Minute accounts of everyday life, his and those about him. A man who worried that he wasn't doing his best. I rush forward to 1956-1957 and read a full account of my beginnings. A full term baby but only five pounds weight at birth, I was born in the yellow room after a day and night of labour. Gertrude, Inga's daughter, was born a week later. My parents gave thanks to my mother's God by paying for Inga's fresh start in Canada.

* * *

Christmas has come and gone. I spent a few days of it at Marge's but would have preferred it on my own. I wanted a solitary Christmas but nobody thought that was good for me. Not Marge, not Mrs Harty. Marge insisted that I stay over with her from Christmas Eve until St Stephen's Day. I had always come home for Christmas. A fact Dad noted with delight in his journal. In recent years Barry came home with me at Christmas time. He revelled in a traditional family Christmas. This year there is a double loss: no parents, no Barry. Greta sent a card signed, Greta, Barry and the girls. The picture showed a roly-poly snowman with a red scarf. She wrote,

Happy Christmas Dee,
We're fine. Got married at Thanksgiving.

I didn't reply. I made a list of what I would and wouldn't have this Christmas. No tree, but I'd put up the crib. Mam and Dad used to decorate the tree with miniature old toys of mine from the nursery. Wooden painted toys of all sorts. Some Dad had made himself and painted, others he'd bought throughout my childhood. There was the Alice collection with most of the characters still intact. The paint on the Mad Hatter's coat was chipped but that was all the damage.

'One of the best stories ever written, Dee. As entertaining for adults as for children,' Dad would say most years when we lined the characters up on the kitchen table to inspect them. 'Written by a mathematician. Isn't that strange! My father wanted me to be an accountant. I had the head but not the stomach for figures.'

'What about the true story of Christmas?' Mam would interject as she dusted her crib figures the other end of the table.

'That's a wonderful story too, of course it is, but for sheer entertainment you can't beat Alice.' Then there were the contents of the doll's house: little people and furniture, so much of it, it filled branch after branch. Mam topped it all off with a beautiful angel in flowing robes of Pender lace. When the tree and crib were in place and decorated, Dad would say,

'I think all that hard work calls for a little refreshment. Who'd like a drink?'

'I'll wait until after midnight mass, John,' she'd say.

'Too much mortification is bad for the soul, Sarah,'

he'd tease. 'It says so in that pamphlet of yours called *There Is A God.*'

'I'll join you, Dad, provided it's straight whiskey.'

We'd have two whiskies each before midnight mass, after I had turned twenty-one, but never more.

'Drink is wonderful in moderation,' was one of his favourite sayings.

I wanted them to stop decorating the tree with toys when I was a teenager and almost said it the Christmas I was sixteen. Greta teased me unmercifully about it.

'You're such a bloody baby, toys on the Christmas tree and you call yourself a teenager!'

It gave Mam and Dad such pleasure, I couldn't bring myself to say it and hurt their feelings. Christmas at Marge and Tom's this year was fine but I had to force myself to be jolly. Tom is one of those dreadful people who feels compelled to organise others into groups or games all the time. I was worn out from playing scrabble, chess, trivial pursuits, not to mention the appalling party games when he and Marge invited the neighbours in on Christmas Eve.

I had invited Hattie to 'Field End' for St Stephen's Day, so I made an early escape from Marge's. I was relieved to slump into a chair in the drawing room and let Mrs Harty wait on Hattie and myself. Mrs Harty had an enormous fire lit and blazing by the time I picked up Hattie from Nash Lodge. Hattie was delighted and spent most of the day looking at its live flames.

'A fireplace with a glowing fire is the centre of a room,' she told us time and again throughout the day.

Sherry was the only drink she'd allow past her lips. She hinted that all other drinks were somehow masculine and on no account to be touched by real ladies. In the event, all three of us got smashed on sherry as we sipped first delicately and then with increasing speed glass after glass as the day progressed towards evening.

It was a day for reminiscences. I read some comic extracts aloud from Dad's journal. One was about the time I drank almost half a bottle of Aunt Alice's home-made blackberry wine. I was six years old and apparently woke up in the middle of the night and made my way down to the pantry. A half dozen bottles of Aunt Alice's wine were maturing there. One of the corks had popped spontaneously and I had sat down on the pantry floor to enjoy its contents. Aunt Em interrupted my enjoyment. My singing and laughter woke her. She woke Aunt Alice, who woke Mam and Dad and all four of them armed themselves with brushes, mops and rolling pins to frighten whatever burglar had disturbed their night's rest. On reaching the pantry, they saw a very happy, drunk toddler, singing and laughing, having a party all on her ownsome.

It's a wonder my little body survived the experience. They rang Dr Caird, who wasn't at all amused at being summoned to the bedside of a legless tot in the small hours. He prescribed milk and sleep; the adults mopped up the mess that followed. Isn't it extraordinary that I don't have any recollection of the experience! It was almost the end of Aunt Alice's home-made wines. Aunt Em proposed their demise on the grounds of health and safety but apparently Dad, Aunt Alice and Mam said a lock on the pantry door would be a more reasonable solution.

The other extract I read dealt with the 'Memory Incident,' so called by Dad in the journal. Aunt Em corrected Aunt Alice on a point of grammar one day. Aunt Alice held her ground.

'Roguery is an abstract noun, Em. Don't you remember your Nesfield's Grammar? An abstract noun denotes some quality, state, or action apart from any object or objects.'

Aunt Em agreed with the definition but said there was no such word as roguery.

'But we learned it in the list, don't you remember?' Aunt Em obviously didn't but she never surrendered easily. Finally, she had to concede when Dad produced the grammar book and pointed to the list, 'cleverness, height, humility, roguery.' After that, any time someone in the house thought Aunt Em was in the wrong they'd say,

'Remember roguery.'

Mrs Harty and Hattie enjoy to the full hearing about these incidents and we toast the memories of the past in another round of sherries. Hattie tells us about the declining fortunes of the Balcombe-Smythes.

'Poor Hermione, nothing left but the house and yard and forty acres. She should have him locked up. I know I would.'

She's talking about Hermione's husband, a ne'er do well and a drunk.

'She's had to take in . . . people,' she lowers her voice to an almost whisper.

'People?' Mrs Harty requires clarification. There's a long silence. I wonder if Hattie has fallen asleep. The room is stiflingly warm by now. The heat and the sherry, I think, have put her to sleep. 'Paying guests, she calls them. Country house holidays. Some such nonsense. Her father must be turning in his grave. Strangers sleeping in his bed. A disgrace! She says her hands are tied. Two of the boys are still at school, you see.'

'I think it's a lovely way to make a living. I'm sure she meets lots of interesting people.' Mrs Harty is immune to Hattie's shock.

'Quite,' Hattie rejoins severely, 'but people like Hermione aren't cut out for making a living. They need to be looked after.'

'Needs must when the devil drives,' Mrs Harty muses philosophically and all three of us stare into the dancing flames of the Christmas fire, mute witches. Later on, Harty drives Hattie back to Nash Lodge. I'm too drunk to drive. Mrs Harty and I hang over the dying embers stoking memories. Later still in bed I howl my desolation into the pillow. Last Christmas, Mam, Dad and Barry were here. Now I'm on my own.

I've stayed put here in 'Field End' these past few months apart from day trips to Dublin or Cork city. A cloistered life, but it's what I needed. So much has changed in the world in that short time. The Wall has come down in Germany. Lisa sent me her article celebrating the event with a photograph of herself amongst hundreds drinking champagne at the Brandenburg Gate. She sent me a lump of the wall as a Christmas gift. Ann hasn't returned to Oregon. She sent me a folk dancer's costume. She's training to become an English language guide in Budapest. Does this mean she really is a spy? Lisa says all spies have not been recalled to base yet. So much for the new freedom! Still, Hungarians had a happy Christmas.

Church bells rang and families united in true celebration, in many cases for the first time since 1956.

In Romania they're still fighting it out on the streets. Ceaucescu's dead, his death and the horrors of his regime in Romania flickered across our Christmas TV screens. Students and workers are fighting for freedom. Many are dying. After fifty years there is a free press. Pictures of soldiers reading the three new daily papers flash by on the news, interspersed with the sounds of Securitate snipers. There is live coverage of one of Ceaucescu's secret policemen being hunted down in Timisoara. Documentaries reveal more. Abject poverty, abandoned children, poor housing and hospitals. There is a special programme on childless Irish parents who are flying out to Bucharest to adopt abandoned children as soon as the fighting ends. I flick through Dad's journal to the copybook with the newspaper cuttings. An article with the headline, MANY OFFERS TO ADOPT CHILDREN, relates how the Irish Red Cross Society had over five hundred applications to adopt Hungarian children in December 1956. Are they all Irish adults now? How differently Dad's four-part little journal reads to me now. I've learned a lot about myself this winter.

I've spent most of that time completing the first draft of my book on Emily Dickinson and reading and re-reading Dad's diary, endless copybooks. Fifty-two years of his life documented. It's all there. The first apple, the last daffodil. Mam's many pregnancies and miscarriages, my birth, my first step. So many of my firsts. My lessons with Miss Bateman. Mrs Harty's recipe for Queen of Puddings, his favourite. And of course, Knocklasheelin Camp, Inga's story, the birth of her daughter, Gertrude, their new life in Canada. Mam's health is recorded in minute detail. His lack of Catholic belief is set down next to detailed descriptions of Mam's devotion to St Gertrude, the foreign saint who eventually brought the safe arrival of a daughter. Dad is amazed but also touched by her simple belief.

The copybooks hold litanies of joys and sorrows. His father Daniel's disappointment in him, his own disappointment in himself as a businessman. According to these notes, Aunts Em and Alice really ran the business until cousin Tom's regime. Dad was a figurehead, a man whose name appeared on the stationery. He went to his office from ten until three, then came home to be with Mam and me. I didn't know until much later in life that most fathers would have spent very little time at home with their families in the fifties and early sixties. The only fathers I knew then were Dad and Harty. Harty was at home permanently.

It's all here. Over fifty years of his life and all of my life at home. Others too. Arguments with Aunt Em over all manner of things from the organisation of the business to bizarre domestic organisation. Apparently she thought floor mops were an indulgence and scrubbing brushes and soap were what was needed. Dad bought the mops and Mam, Mrs Harty and himself hid them in an attic cupboard. Mrs Harty mopped the floors on Wednesdays when Aunt Em ate at the Butler Arms. I ask Mrs Harty about this and she roars with laughter.

'Took me nearly a full month after they laid your Aunt Em in the soil before I could bring myself to store my mops downstairs. We were all terrified of her, even Mr Pender. She was good in other ways, I'll give her that. Put shoes on my children's feet every Christmas, she did. Good leather ones too, from Finerty's shop.'

Alice's damson jam. She filled the pantry shelves with it one year, the year she almost married Michael Wilmot. It didn't work out. Em didn't think him good enough. Wore Alice down until she agreed and she never made damson jam again. All through the years in these pages, Dad describes in loving detail every dress, blouse and handkerchief Mam made. Marge is going to use sections from the diary to document Mam's lacework at the museum. We've photocopied and mounted the ones she wanted. They're at the framer's for suitably old-fashioned frames. Mam used to listen at the door during Miss Bateman's lessons. Knowing this now reduces those classes to comic proportions. When I look at the malnourished abandoned Romanian children on news bulletins, their eyes staring as if unseeing, Miss Bateman assumes diminutive proportions, a kindly irritant.

I have continued my cleaning routine. It's gone beyond the therapy stage. I've come to love each vase, each picture that belongs here. Other routines have become ritualised too. I sit in the greenhouse for a quarter of an hour in the early evenings in spite of the cold. I wear one of Dad's tweed jackets when I go out there. I gave Tom Burke the rest of them. At first he didn't want to take them but I assured him that's what Dad would have wanted. I time my entrance to the greenhouse with the end of Tom's working day. He goes home at five each day. I sit down and read through a few pages of one of the copybooks with a torch. It's still quite dark in the early evenings. Makes Dad seem closer. Harty is bending his back in Dad's good suits these days. Mrs Harty brought them to Will Barrett to adjust them to Harty's size. It's cold but I don't mind. January, a new year, a new month, a new start.

Irina sends new year's greetings.

Dear Dee,
Draft one is reasonable. Two publishers are interested. I told them you'll have the revised manuscript by Easter. Start draft two now.
Irina.

I miss my students and my teaching on days when the writing is slow or difficult. Hattie has been pestering me about Dad's copies. Marge says, 'Hattie has got nothing to do with it, it's a family affair.' I visit Hattie twice a week, Tuesdays and Thursdays usually at four thirty precisely. We sit either side of her unlit fire and I read her another instalment from the copies. We've both become rather addicted. I read for an hour, then we chat. Or at least, she talks and I listen. She took particular and partial delight in Dad's detailed account of 'the Canon's Appeal'. Dad had written a full account of Mrs Harty's mother's accident and her death three months later. He kept the newspaper cutting of the result of the appeal. It read:

CANON APPEALS AGAINST £1,500 JURY AWARD
The Supreme Court gave judgement yesterday in an appeal in an action which had been heard at the High Court on Circuit in Cork.
The appeal was from the verdict of a jury and judgement for £1,500 for Mrs Grace Meehan, housewife, Ballinane Cottages, Cork, in an action taken by her against the Very Rev. James Murray, Dublin, claiming damages for

injuries.

It was stated that while walking across a zebra crossing in front of Canon Murray's church on April 14th 1964 Mrs Meehan was struck by a motor car owned by Canon Murray and that she had suffered injury to the back.
Mr W Fitzpatrick, SC, Mr Oliver Grogan, SC and Mr F O'Brien (instructed by Messrs Rushbrook and Co) appeared for Canon Murray. Mr J O'Connor, SC, Mr K Buckley, SC and Mr C Moloney (instructed by Messrs Simms and Co) appeared for Mrs Meehan.

Mr Fitzpatrick submitted that on the evidence the case should have been withdrawn from the jury. The court found in favour of the appellant, Canon Murray. Dad records his disappointment that a clergyman would not face up to his responsibilities in this matter. 'Very Roman,' Hattie chuckles. 'Their clergy seem to be able to forgive themselves the most appalling shortcomings without batting an eyelid. We had a little downstairs maid at Topayne House. She was Catholic. When she had been with us for about three months, her priest paid her a visit. The mistress gave her the use of the downstairs parlour to talk to him. Mrs Balcombe-Smythe was very civilised. After ten minutes, little Helen came out of the room all tear-stained and blushing. Do you know what the purpose of the visit was?'

'To warn her of the sins of the flesh or check her attendance at mass.'

'Not a bit of it. He had visited her to remind her that she hadn't handed in her envelope for the Cathos Campaign since coming to his parish. At first, we had no idea what this campaign meant.'

'Planned giving,' I say 'is another word for it, an envelope with money inside it for the support of the parish, handed in at Sunday mass.'

'Quite. This man of God came to tell Helen that she was a thoughtless sinner because she wasn't putting God and his church first, in importance, in her weekly budget.' Hattie's room is powerfully heated and I feel quite faint and thirsty by the time I've finished reading, not to mention paying attention to her spirited talk. We have tea from her Duchess china set, the one Aunt Alice left her and eat a Mrs Harty special, usually brown scones with jam and a cake or pie to follow. Hattie urges me towards publication of Dad's diary and resists my efforts to explain market forces. Tom is outraged at the very thought of publication.

'It gave Uncle something to do, filled in his leisure time.'

'You're afraid I'll publish the ones about your takeover, aren't you?'

'No, not at all,' he splutters his protest.

In the Autumn copies for 1967 Dad gives a full account of Tom's takeover of the business. There are one or two incidents that should make Tom blush. I'm enjoying his discomfort.

Mrs Harty and I have become friends. I still call her Mrs Harty. Habit persists. It's a shock when I realise that she's only fifty. I'm thirty-two, same age as Greta. The shadow of Greta's pregnancy looms between us but we avoid talking directly about it.

'Sure I was only an innocent eighteen year old when Greta was born. I had learned a lot by the time Lally came.'

The three of us, Mrs Harty, Lally and myself go to

Cork city once a week to shop. Saturday morning we set off to be in the city by nine. Mrs Harty now has a grudging respect for 'Emily' and no longer refers to her in derogatory terms. She buys groceries for the week and I browse in the bookshops. Lally moves between bookshops and grocery shops and we have lunch out before driving back to 'Field End'. Lally has no interest in *Alice in Wonderland* and *Alice Through the Looking Glass*. I show her Dad's large collection of the many editions of the books. He belonged to the 'Alice Club'. They sent him regular newsletters. A bookcase in his study overflows with various editions. She's unimpressed.

'A man reading children's books! Imagine buying the same two books over and over.'

Her reading interest is centred on fact, biography, history, big events, great lives.

Nothing is said directly about my intentions at the end of my sabbatical but it's on Mrs Harty's mind. From time to time she'll say, 'Of course, you'd never stick the quiet life here, not after the hurly burly of New York.' I neither agree nor disagree. A thought has been taking root over these past few weeks since Christmas. A plan. Inspired by Hattie's story of Hermione Balcome-Smythe who has turned Topayne House into a country house for guests to make a living, I've begun wondering if the same could be done at 'Field End'. Of course there's no comparison between the two houses, except for period — they're both Georgian. Topayne House is large and beautiful on the grand scale, formal gardens set in forty acres, hard and grass tennis courts, a lake for boating and fishing and well-run stables.

Belonging

I've begun to feel a responsibility towards 'Field End' I never felt before. I love Mam's lacework now in a way that was impossible for me to do when she was alive. Dad I have come to understand better through the diaries. A courageous timid man is how I sum him up these days. What happens when I go back to New York at the end of next August? Selling the place has long since left my head. I couldn't wait to get away from here after college, to explore the new, the unfamiliar. These days I take a pleasure in it that's mixed with nostalgia, yes, but also new delight. As I move about the house I know exactly what's in it. My clearing and cleaning phase has ended, much to the relief of Mrs Harty, I think, though she hasn't voiced any feelings on the matter. Six boxes of stuff were put in the attic, but that's all. The rest has been cleaned and put back in the usual places.

I find pleasure in looking through Dad's binoculars and trying on Mam's hats. This is 'playing house' but much more too. I walk the four fields, Bluebell, Horsefield, Giant's Stone and Field End and I feel a sense of territory, of belonging, that's strong and positive. I know I will not be able to turn my back on that feeling easily.

The plan has grown from the daydream stage into something more tangible. 'Field End' is not a large house by any means but it is roomy. It has five bedrooms. An Irish Georgian country house, my home, my place. But I work in New York. I've lived there for the last decade. I love my work. Teaching is important to me. There is no way that I could get a comparable teaching post in Ireland. What to do? I talked about it to Marge and she thinks 'Field End' could work quite well for country house holidays provided the necessary renovations are tackled properly. She has been quite worried about Dad's diary and what I plan to do with it.

'Unpublishable,' I say over the phone. 'If I did tighten it up for publication, then it wouldn't be Dad's anymore. No, I'm having the copybooks bound and I'll put them on the open shelves in his study. That's where they belong.'

Tom's reaction to the news is one of overwhelming jocularity. He welcomes me back into the family fold. They invite me to Sunday lunch and after two sherries Tom says, 'Such a relief. It would have been in foul taste of course, but I'm glad you've changed your mind.'

He refills my glass, and taps me awkwardly on the back as if he's burping a child.

'I haven't changed my mind,' I say. 'I knew after the first reading it was unpublishable.'

'But after all these months,' he protests.

'Hattie was the one who talked of publication,' I remind him.

'Poor Marge has been off her food and I've not been sleeping properly. The business. It could have tarnished the image of Pender glass and lace . . . we were worried.'

I look across at Marge. She has lost weight these past few months. There's a drawn look to that fine face. The green eyes look dull. Trapped, somehow.

'I haven't been worried about Uncle's diary. It's Sam. He's ill,' she sips her sherry and makes a face as if it's a bitter, medicinal drink.

'What nonsense, Marge, he looked splendid last

summer,' Tom booms. 'You worry too much. I wish he wouldn't write about every chill and cough.'

Marge puts down her sherry glass carefully on the table.

'He's ill, really ill,' her voice seems hoarse. 'He's in hospital with pneumonia at the moment. He doesn't know when he'll get out.'

'He'll be fine . . . will I give Dash a run before lunch, Marge?'

'If you like.'

And Tom is out the door whistling Dash to heel, leaving Marge and me to each other. We stare into our glasses. Sam's ill-health crowds the room.

'Tom's a fine man really. A good husband and father in lots of ways.'

There's an interminable silence. I examine the silly hunting prints on the wall and the delicate cracks on a large vase that holds silk white roses on top of the fireplace.

'I wish Greta was here,' Marge says. 'She knows how to make the best of everything.'

'Yes, she does,' I agree reluctantly, 'but you're an expert at that yourself.'

'I've had to become one, I suppose. Tom's talents are for business. He likes things to be black and white. If I feel down it makes him uncomfortable.'

'You could ring Greta,' I suggest.

'Yes, I could but she's enough on her plate at the moment.'

'The baby's due in another few weeks, isn't it?'

'Easter Sunday, in fact,' Marge says.

'You've been in contact with her then?'

'I write once a month as usual. Always have.'

Marge and Sam's lists! In cutting off contact with Greta I'd assumed everyone else had too. Absurd now when I think of it because from time to time Lally had let slip little tit-bits of news.

'Cáit and Róisín hope it's a girl. They want a sister.'

'Ma told Harty about Greta's baby. He said she's a rip. Greta, not Ma.'

But I'd put them to the back of my mind, deliberately leaving them in darkness. I didn't feel strong enough to put my feelings on the matter under minute examination.

'She's not having an easy time of it,' Marge continues in those quiet uninflected tones of hers. 'The girls don't want to leave the school they attend in their neighbourhood and Barry doesn't want to leave his apartment. Neither apartment is big enough for all of them together, so she lives with the girls in her apartment during the week and they all go to Barry's at the weekend.'

'A weekend marriage. It works for the movie stars. Anyway she knew what she was getting into.' I'm surprised at my own bitterness.

'You haven't forgiven her?'

'No. Could you?'

'Maybe not.'

'Sandysocks, yes. This, no.'

'Sandysocks! But surely she had nothing to do with that. It was an accident. A fire in the middle of the night. Nobody's fault.'

'She told Dad. Not then, not when it happened. Years later. At her wedding reception, when she married the Voiceover. It's in the diary.'

'But that's dreadful.'

'She hadn't intended it to go so far. A little fire. Enough to upset Sandysocks, to stop him jumping the following week. It took us longer to wake up than she'd calculated. She was only nine at the time. She really loved Sandysocks. It's hard to streamline time and motion at that stage.'

'Then why did she do it? She loved him as much as you did. Spent hours grooming him and mucking out his stable.'

'I owned him. She didn't. It was as simple and as complex as that. Jealousy.'

'It's one of the easiest emotions to feel. I was jealous too. Not of you exactly, but what you had.'

'But we shared everything!'

'You shared everything with Sam and me and Greta.'

'I didn't know you felt like that.'

'Uncle was always kind. Paid for riding lessons at Carduignan for Sam and me. Gave us tasteful presents at Christmas and birthdays, had us to tea once a week.'

'But you loved Mrs Harty's "teas fit for princesses".'

'Of course I did. But it was on your territory. Uncle's terms. He gave, we took. It's harder sometimes to be at the receiving end.'

'I wanted to be like you and Sam. So assured, no stutters. Everything planned out.'

'I wanted to have two parents like you. Mammy did her best. We got graveyard visits to our Dad once a month. I still find it difficult to believe in heaven. I'm talking too much. It's the sherry and I'm worried about Sam.'

'People clam up or open the floodgates when they're worried. At least that is what Mark says.'

'Who's Mark?'

'My shrink. Or was. I've deserted him. The gospel according to Mark. But even he, on occasion, can be right, I suppose. Tom made a quick exit.'

'He thinks doing a routine task is good for the soul. He's a very straightforward person. I used to admire that in him.'

'Don't worry about Sam. He'll be fine.'

'You're probably right but I had a nightmare about him last night. I can't get it out of my mind. Tom thinks I'm silly paying attention to dreams.'

'Was it bad, the dream?'

'Quite grim. I dreamed Sam was in a cave and a group of men outside it were blocking up the entrance. I couldn't warn him that he wouldn't be able to get out. I was so disturbed by the dream I was going to ring the hospital this morning but I only rang two days ago and he was doing okay. I don't want to worry him either.'

'It's hard to know what's best sometimes. I'm sure he'll be fine. It's probably an anxiety dream. You were anxious about him, so you had a bad dream. You wake up and the dream makes you feel worse. It's a vicious circle. I have terrible dreams about Barry and Greta.'

'Tell me one,' her green eyes enlarge with curiosity but I won't be drawn.

'No. They're too shameful and violent. I don't want to talk about them. They've been getting worse recently, probably because the baby is due soon. It's on my mind but I want to escape from it. I might go to Budapest at Easter.'

She's alarmed but she's trying to conceal it.

'I thought Uncle's diaries had cleared up all of that.'

'They have but I'd like to get away for a bit and I won't have much free time once the renovations on the house start. I've an American friend who lives in Budapest, a journalist. I could do with a holiday and I know Mrs Harty is anxious about Greta and the baby. She has to stop herself talking about her sometimes. If I'm out of the way when the baby's born, it will be easier for everyone. After Easter we'll have to get organised with builders and painters. The house is sound structurally but it's quite shabby. Needs lots of paint and some of the furniture will have to be re-upholstered. And then there are the extra bathrooms that will have to be put in.'

'You're not having second thoughts about your own plans for the house then? I thought you might change your mind again.'

'No. It's what I want. I've done all the basic research. Country house accommodation with Mrs Harty as chef. April to October opening.' And I reel off the facilities like an advertisement. 'Maximum capacity, five doubles. Small scale stuff but exciting nonetheless.'

'You'll have to renovate properly.'

'Bathrooms for each guestroom but that's all. I don't want to destroy its character.'

'I'll help you get a brochure out. We can stress the amenities nearby, golf, riding, fishing. You'll need a manager and a small staff. I know all the locals.'

'I finish my lectures by mid May and start teaching again in October, so it should work well.'

'Nothing's perfect. It's hard work dealing with people, believe me, but if you get a good staff you'll be okay. 'Field End' has enough charm to seduce anyone.'

I reveal my plans to Mrs Harty when I get home from Marge's. She's pleased, nervous, excited, overwhelmed, all in one. 'Will I be up to the responsibility? That's my main worry. A hotel!'

'Country house accommodation,' I amend. 'After all we have only five bedrooms. Something intimate but cheerful. Marge recommended the Duignan brothers for the renovations. What do you think?'

'Slow, but good workers. They leave no mess and that's important.'

'We've loads of time. A year before opening. Just think, Mrs Harty, teas fit for princesses every afternoon.'

* * *

I fly to Budapest on Good Friday, three days before Greta's baby is due. Mrs Harty, Lally and Harty see me off at the airport. Lisa meets me when I land. I'm grateful. The airport is crowded and there are long queues for taxis. She has to park a little distance from Vatci Utca as it's a pedestrian street. We pass a tourist information bureau and there are long queues of people there too. 'Everyone had the same idea this Easter, let's go to Budapest,' Lisa says as we pass the Ibusz, 'but I'm glad you're here.'

Her flat overlooks the street and is directly opposite a bookshop called *The Owl Bookshop*. It sells English as well as Hungarian books. The flat is compact, two bedrooms, a bathroom and kitchen. The gas stove is tiny, of antique age. 'Does it work?'

'Perfectly, but I don't cook much.'

The furniture is modern, functionally ugly, a table, some chairs and a couch. A portable TV, a shelf of books and a violin complete the decor.

'I know it's ugly but I don't spend much time in it,'

she says as she watches my reconaissant glance.

We eat out at a little restaurant quite close to the Gellert hotel. I'm too tired to eat much but I drink several glasses of a good white wine. On the way home I notice most of the shop windows are decorated with Easter eggs. They're painted in bright colours in a variety of patterns, symmetrical and stylized motifs: sunflowers, butterflies, tiny horse-shoes.

'The women and girls paint them,' Lisa says. 'Fertility rites,' she laughs.

We stop at a confectioner's window that is spilling over with eggs. Their colours and painted patterns dance in the harsh light. My eyes seek out the eggs that have little horseshoes on them. Baby eggs. We press our noses to the glass like children. We walk to Vorosmarty square and have our portraits drawn by street artists. Next morning when I examine my charcoal drawing in detail, it seems to me that the artist has given me goitrous eyes. They bulge out at me.

The week's holiday goes very quickly. Lisa has to work every morning but she's free in the afternoons. We go to Heroes' Square and she photographs me next to the huge statues of the Magyar tribes on horseback. We try to make the soldiers who are on duty laugh. They are standing rigidly to attention. Not a smirk. Young men in green uniforms with a ribbon of red around their caps, rifles held at the ready in white-gloved hands, they remain impassive and will not talk to us. Lisa talks in halting Hungarian to the two cleaners wheeling their barrow of dirt through the square. Their brooms are primitive, witchlike.

Ann is back in Oregon at a folkdancing festival but Lisa shows me the building where her office is. It's next door to a Lutheran church. Organ music reaches the street. Bach, I think.

'There's nothing left to spy on. I don't know what the hell she's still here for. It's all openness and sharing secrets these days.'

There are MDF election posters everywhere. A pregnant woman in a blue-print dress, with long flowing red hair, looks out at us and to Hungary's future from the poster. 'Sweet, isn't it?' Lisa says.

'Greta's baby is due today,' I remind myself and tell Lisa.

'I don't know what to say about that. I guess you must be feeling pretty low.'

'I've been pushing it to the side of my head all winter. It took me until Christmas to realise that there was going to be a baby and now the Easter bunny will bring a baby as sure as eggs are eggs.'

'But they told you about it the end of August.'

'Yea, I know, but I really didn't accept it until I was dusting down the baby figure to put in the crib at Christmas. What can I say! I'm a late developer.'

The days pass. Mornings, when Lisa is at the office, I travel from one part of the city to the other by tram and bus. I'm not scared of getting lost like I was last summer. The loud noise of the trams doesn't bother me. I'm relaxed but directionless. I look about me but I'm looking for nothing in particular. One day, I go to the last tram stop on the line and end up in a seemingly never-ending lakotelep development. I wonder if it's the same one I visited last summer with Lisa. I think of Granny, Judit, Gertrude and the three men named Janos. What are they doing now?

I return to the city and wander into a market. The

stalls are piled high with paprika, garlic, fruits and very fat meats, pork, I think. I sit on a park bench and smile at anyone who passes by. I spend another morning going up and down the Danube by boat.

Lisa organises the afternoons and evenings. We go to a poetry reading at the Astoria on Wednesday but I urge defection at the interval. Another time we go to a premier of a film. It's avant-garde collage, a jumble of disturbing images and loud music but at least it's short. At the reception afterwards, Lisa introduces me to the director and most of the actors. They're intense young people. Beautiful to look at but exhausting to concentrate on for conversation purposes. They have so little English, I have no Hungarian, so I'm thrown back on energetic body language to emphasise any point I try to make. On my final evening we go to a piano recital. A medley of modern and classical music, quite soothing. We have a supper of bread and cheese washed down with champagne.

'Didn't I tell you lives are simple?'

'So you did,' I agree.

'Bread, cheese and a drink, you can't beat it.'

'Greta, Barry and baby, that's certainly beat me,' I giggle. I'm slightly drunk.

'At least you won't have to learn Hungarian, now that you know you are who you are. Not like me. I'm a hybrid.'

'A what?'

'A hybrid, neither one thing, nor the other. I ran away from the music world and some days I want to run away from journalism. We live in a sordid world.'

'What do you want to run towards?'

'Dunno. Maybe nothing. Maybe music without the

pressures of the solo circuit but I haven't figured out a way of doing that yet.'

'I haven't figured out how to deal with Greta's baby yet.'

I don't see Lisa the following morning when I leave. She's already at the office. A note propped on the kitchen table reads:

Bye. Lisa.

Harty meets me at the airport. He's wearing one of Dad's grey suits. After we've exchanged pleasantries about travel and weather he says, 'It's a boy, eight pounds, Fionn.'

He looks me in the eye, then turns his head away sharply. He picks up my suitcase and sets a cracking pace to the car. He doesn't speak again until we're halfway home.

'It's a thunderin' disgrace, but sure the poor child is an innocent.'

Fionn. A name to grow into and live up to! Trust Greta. A baby giant steps forward.

Mark writes,

Dear Dee,
I ran into your actress friend Greta last week. She had a tiny baby in a sling. Said it's Barry's. I guess we've both had a rough time this past year. Greta says you are coming back to New York this Fall. I think you should see me.
Mark.

I write,

Dear Mark,
Goodbye Bully.
Deirdre.

Lisa writes,
Dear Dee,
I've located Inga Kadir through a CIA contact. These guys can find anyone. She lives on Mignonne St, Ontario. She's been married twice to the same guy, Janos. He seems to be the one who was in the camp with her. He's a carpenter. They live apart. She's made a fortune on real estate. Three kids, Gertrude (thirty-three this March), in business with her mother, Paul (thirty), a musician, and Marie Therese (twenty-five) who works in a government office.
You want to make contact?
Lisa.

I write,
Dear Lisa,
I didn't realise you'd follow through on all this when I'd dropped it. Thanks but I've decided to let living ghosts lie. The builders are in! Noise and dirt everywhere but it will be worth it in the end, or so they say. I go back to New York in early August. I don't want to clash with Greta's annual visit home. I'm working flat out on my book.
Dee.
PS Why don't you take some leave and come here? July would be perfect.

Greta writes,
Dear Dee,
How are you? I believe you've great plans for 'Field End' and you've started the renovations. Barry, the kids and myself will be over as usual in August. Have you seen the Voiceover's new film? Naked bodies everywhere. Fionn is a little marvel, a great eater and sleeper.
Love,
Greta.

'She can't stay here. None of them can.' I'm pacing the kitchen, the postcard in my hand.

'No, of course not,' Mrs Harty soothes, 'and Harty won't have her in the house. It'll have to be the Butler Arms.'

So much for letting living ghosts lie! But then courage doesn't come in giant proportions. I know I can't block out what's happened between Greta, Barry and me, but it will have to wait. I'll feel better able to handle it when I'm back in New York. It's May again. I've been here a year. I make a May altar for Mam, light candles and put lilac in vases. I fill Dad's fountain pen and write THE END at the end of my typed manuscript on Emily Dickinson.

I send a postcard to Greta.

Dear Greta,
I'll have left by the time you arrive in August. I'm sure you'll find your stay in the Butler Arms comfortable.
Dee.

* * *

4
A NEW APARTMENT

IT IS MID DECEMBER. Outside, New York snow builds but it cannot cushion the sound of traffic. Since my return I find myself writing intermittently in this diary. Not every day. Sometimes not even every week but at regular intervals nonetheless. After a few days back at college, it felt like I had never been away. Classes, meetings and students filled my days. Finding a suitable apartment took longer than that and was exhausting. My replacement, Anna, offered me a room in her apartment until I found a place of my own. An offer that I found curious since my return should signal her demise, but not so. A new post has been created for her — she teaches a combination of elementary composition and Modern European Poetry. Hence the hospitality. I accepted. My college life assumed order and shape almost immediately. My leisure time proved more problematic.

I do two hours voluntary work on Tuesdays and Thursdays at the Central European Resettlement programme in the city but apart from that I do not see many people. A year is a long time to be away and I found it took me quite a while to adjust once more to the busyness and noise of the New York streets. Apart from that I found myself haunted by memories of

Barry when I passed familiar parts of the city we'd made our own. Friends I thought we had shared had in my absence absorbed Greta and the children into their lives and it was plain to me that they had come down on Barry's side and that I was now the outsider.

Music in particular is difficult for me now. That was the main interest we had in common. I have boxed and stored most of the tapes we played when we were together. My hand faltered over the Stirkov tape as I packed the boxes. And I didn't pack it away. I keep it in my office in college but I have not played it. I haven't avoided the Irish Arts Centre but I time my attendance at events with the care of a convalescent patient. I've been lucky. I haven't bumped into Barry and Greta there yet. I miss going to the theatre with Greta. She has a good role in a relatively successful play in an off-off Broadway production at the moment. The college kids love it. Greta plays the part of an abandoned Romanian child raised in one of Ceaucescu's asylums. Everyone thinks she's retarded as she's been locked up for twenty years. In fact she's been writing poetry secretly all this time and the poems speak with an intelligent confidence that's astounding. I went to see it with Anna. Greta was perfect in the role. I sent a note and some flowers but I could not bring myself to go backstage.

I moved into this apartment last month. It has one bedroom, a kitchen, bathroom and small living room. I painted all the walls yellow. The fittings are made of light ash wood. The apartment gives the impression of great warmth. I have chosen what I put into it with great care. The copper kettle from 'Field End' and Aunt Alice's white delph in the kitchen. In the living room a reproduction of Paula Modersohn-Becker's 'Self Portrait on Sixth Anniversary'. It's a quiet painting. The artist wears her long hair in tight coils on her head. She wears a brown necklace and a white half slip. The slip starts at the hips. Her breasts and tummy are exposed. Her right hand lies across her waist, the left one cups her pregnant belly. The other reproduction is a portrait of the twelfth century Abbess Hildegaard Von Bingen, visionary, poet and composer. A late starter — at forty-three, tongues of fire descended on her in a vision and inspired her to take up the creative arts.

These pictures and my books are all I want in the living room. In the bedroom, I have yellow bed linen and curtains. The wardrobe, a modern functional one, fits all my clothes easily and there's room to spare. I know I will be able to work well in this apartment. Its clear bright lines encourage me to simplicity and clarity. I have begun to write fiction. Short stories. I write them down in hardbacked copybooks and leave them. As yet, I haven't re-read any of them. They write themselves or so it appears to me. I do not want to interrupt their wholeness.

END